# "I Want To Take You To Bed And Break Down All The Barriers You Put Between Us."

"Tad, go away."

"Why?"

"Because I'm not the girl you want."

"Yes, you are."

"Because I like the same Christmas tree you do."

He gave her a half smile that took her breath away. "No, because you're beautiful and sexy and you've haunted my dreams since the last time I saw you."

She took the tray and left the living room. She couldn't think when he said things like that. When he made her believe that forever and happily ever after might still exist. It was as if everything her ex-lover and ex-boss had taught her disappeared. But she knew better.

"I'm not your dream woman, Tad. I'm no man's."

Dear Reader,

Thank you for choosing Silhouette Desire—where passion is guaranteed in every read. Things sure are heating up with our continuing series DYNASTIES: THE BARONES. Eileen Wilks's *With Private Eyes* is a powerful romance that helps set the stage for the daring conclusion next month. And if it's more continuing stories that you want—we have them. TEXAS CATTLEMAN'S CLUB: THE STOLEN BABY launches this month with Sara Orwig's *Entangled with a Texan.*

The wonderful Peggy Moreland is on hand to dish up her share of Texas humor and heat with *Baby, You're Mine,* the next installment of her TANNERS OF TEXAS series. Be sure to catch Peggy's Silhouette Single Title, *Tanner's Millions,* on sale January 2004. Award-winning author Jennifer Greene marks her much-anticipated return to Silhouette Desire with *Wild in the Field,* the first book in her series THE SCENT OF LAVENDER.

Also for your enjoyment this month, we offer Katherine Garbera's second book in the KING OF HEARTS series. *Cinderella's Christmas Affair* is a fabulous "it could happen to you" plot guaranteed to leave her fans extremely satisfied. And rounding out our selection of delectable stories is *Awakening Beauty* by Amy J. Fetzer, a steamy, sensational tale.

More passion to.you!

*Melissa Jeglinski*

Melissa Jeglinski
Senior Editor, Silhouette Desire

Please address questions and book requests to:
Silhouette Reader Service
U.S.: 3010 Walden Ave., P.O. Box 1325, Buffalo, NY 14269
Canadian: P.O. Box 609, Fort Erie, Ont. L2A 5X3

# Cinderella's Christmas Affair

## KATHERINE GARBERA

Published by Silhouette Books
**America's Publisher of Contemporary Romance**

SILHOUETTE BOOKS

ISBN 0-373-76546-0

CINDERELLA'S CHRISTMAS AFFAIR

Copyright © 2003 by Katherine Garbera

This edition published by arrangement with Harlequin Books S.A.

Visit Silhouette at www.eHarlequin.com

**Printed in U.S.A.**

## KATHERINE GARBERA

lives in central Florida with her husband and two children. They are all happy to be back in their native state after a two-year absence. Her favorite things are spending time with her family, writing, reading and talking about reading. Readers can visit her on the Web at katherinegarbera.com.

To Courtney, Lucas and Matt—
thanks for making everything worthwhile.

Acknowledgments:

Special thanks to Julie Wachowski
for suggesting Gejas as a romantic place for dinner.
Also, thanks to the entire Windy City chapter
for being so knowledgeable about everything
and for making me feel like one of your own
even it was only for a short time.

# Prologue

**D**ying had not been what I'd expected and after successfully matching together one couple I felt a little more confident about this afterlife gig. But this body disappearing thing still freaked me out. I was back in that in-between land that Father Dom had called purgatory.

I'd been a capo in the mob before being betrayed by one of my lieutenants. Five shots to the chest and a dying request for forgiveness had brought me here.

The deal I'd cut was essentially to unite in love as many couples as enemies I'd murdered in hate. So I knew I'd be dealing with this angel broad for a while. Matchmaker to the lovelorn wasn't exactly something I'd been dying to do but life was full of surprises. Come to think of it so was death.

In front of me was a large mahogany desk with a library lamp and a jar of Baci chocolates. I'd been here before. The angel broad was there, still looking like she'd just attended a funeral but her dress this time was puke-green.

She was making notes in a file folder. She didn't glance up and I knew she was playing a game with me. I'd done the same thing a time or two when I'd been a capo. It made me feel like a *cugine* instead of the boss of bosses, which I'd essentially been. I didn't like it.

"What's up next, babe?" I asked.

"Mr. Mandetti, unless you want me to stop this whole exercise now, you will refrain from calling me babe."

I still wasn't used to being called by my real name. I'd been *Il Re* when I was alive. *The King*. Yeah, I had an ego and the attitude to carry off that name. "I don't know your name."

"Didiero. I'm one of the seraphim."

"The what?"

"One of the highest angels of God."

"Oh." She made me feel stupid which wasn't a feeling I liked. But she held all the cards and if I'd learned one thing from my time back on earth it was that I didn't want to go to hell.

And I'd never admit this to anyone but I liked the feeling that came with doing something good. It was the first time I'd ever experienced it.

"Didi?" I asked.

"Are you talking to me?" She didn't look up from the papers in front of her.

"Didiero is a mouthful."

She glanced at me from under her lashes. This one would drive me crazy if I let her.

"So who's next?" I asked.

"You still want to go in order?" she asked.

"Nah, give me that green one halfway down." Maybe the middle of the pile would be easier. I wasn't trusting her to pull out a couple. I'm sure she'd fixed it so I'd had to work hard on my first assignment.

She handed me the folder. I opened it up and groaned. CJ Terrence and Tad Randolph. "Aren't there any couples who can do this on their own?"

"Sure, there are Mandetti, but they don't need your help. There is one thing I should warn you about," Didi said.

"Yeah?" I was leery. Why was she suddenly being all helpful?

"You won't take the same human form each time."

It was like she knew how to push my buttons. "Babe, get to the point."

"That is my point, Mandetti."

She disappeared and I felt my body dissolve. I found myself on the streets of Chicago. *My kind of town.* This assignment was looking up by the moment. I was in front of the Michigan Building on Michigan Ave. In the mirrored glass I saw an old lady and two sharp-looking guys.

*Not bad.* I could definitely handle being a young

hip guy. Both of them were taller than I'd been. I walked toward the glass and noticed only the old lady was moving.

*Madon'* that couldn't be me, could it? I gave the reflection the finger. Christ, I was an old broad with a frumpy dress on. Didi was probably up in Heaven laughing. Just wait until I saw her again.

# One

Of course the first man she'd had a crush on would be the only thing standing between her and her promotion. CJ Terrence smiled with a confidence she was far from feeling and shook Tad Randolph's hand.

Ten years had passed since they'd last seen each other and she knew she'd changed a lot. She'd dyed her mousy brown hair a sassy auburn, she'd swapped her horn-rimmed glasses for aqua-colored contacts that masked her natural brown color. And the biggest thing of all, she'd lost twenty pounds.

But in that moment she felt like her former self—the chubby girl next door. She reached for the bridge of her nose to push up the glasses she'd always worn back then. Dropping her hand, she reminded herself that she'd changed.

She took a deep breath; assured herself that her physical changes were enough to keep Tad from recognizing her. Of course, she recognized him even though he'd put on at least twenty pounds. All of it solid muscle. He looked exactly how she'd expect the owner of a sporting goods company to look.

It was too bad he couldn't be balding like other guys who were her age. Instead his blond hair was thick as ever and bleached by the sun. He looked too good and she wanted to run and hide.

"CJ Terrence," she said introducing herself. She could only hope that maybe Tad wouldn't be able to identify her as the girl he'd known as Cathy Jane in high school.

He took her proffered hand and shook it for the required three pumps. Shivers of awareness or maybe it was nerves shook her. His hand was bigger than hers, not surprising since she wasn't a big girl—at five foot five inches tall she was average and Tad Randolph had grown into a giant since she'd last seen him.

Calluses ridged his palm and his skin against hers was rough and warm. She wondered how his hand would feel against her stomach. Tremors of sensual awareness pulsed through her body. He continued to watch her with that razor-sharp gaze of his. Had she given too much away?

"Ms. Terrence, where do you want these presentation boards?" CJ's secretary, Rae-Anne King, asked.

CJ dropped Tad's hand and glanced at her new temporary secretary. "Please excuse me."

"It's a pleasure meeting you, CJ," Tad said.

"I've...got to set up," CJ said. Yes she was the queen of intelligent conversation—not!

"Don't let me keep you."

*Right.* One minute in the man's presence and she'd lost ten years worth of self-confidence. Confidence she'd earned by standing on her own and not depending on anyone else.

Tad nodded and walked to the coffee service that CJ had set up. Normally, her assistant would have handled it but this was her first day working with Rae-Anne. Her temp had proven to be a little inept around the office.

CJ motioned to the easel at the end of the long narrow conference room. Working quickly she set up her presentation and then glanced out the window.

It was a blustery day in early December. Chicago was gray and damp. Though the Christmas decorations along Michigan Avenue tried to instill a little cheer, they failed.

Failure was something CJ understood but she didn't plan to let it rest on her shoulders today. She took a deep breath, muttered her mantra to herself and then turned to face the other people in the room.

Tad touched her shoulder; she started and dropped her cards. *Damn.* This wasn't going to work. Six years of moving her way steadily up in the advertising world was suddenly in jeopardy.

He picked her cards up from the floor and held them out to her. Their hands brushed. His were large and tan. He wrapped his fingers around hers, which were cold. Rubbing his thumb across the back of her knuckles he warmed up more than her fingers.

"Cold hands?" he asked softly.

"Always," she said. Her fingers were never warm even in summer.

"You know what they say about hands," he said.

"Honestly, no."

"Cold hands, warm heart. Do you have a warm heart, CJ?" he asked.

No way was Tad Randolph—the only boy she'd ever allowed herself to have a crush on—flirting with her in the middle of the conference room.

"CJ?"

"Uh…I don't know."

"There's something familiar about you," he said.

She took her cards from his grip and nervously shuffled them. Oh, God, please don't let him remember me. She was never going to be able to do this.

"Have we met?"

She shook her head. God, don't get me for lying, she thought. Just in case she crossed her fingers behind her back. Before she could answer her boss walked in.

"CJ was featured in *Advertising Age* last year as part of their Top Thirty To Watch. Twenty-somethings who were taking the advertising world by storm," Butch Baker said from the doorway.

Butch was forty-eight and had been with Taylor, Banks and Markim forever. He was her immediate boss and observing today as part of the promotion process. CJ was next in line for the directorship of the domestic division of the advertising company. Today's meeting wasn't a make-it or break-it deal, but bagging the sporting goods contract would give her a nice lead over her competition.

Butch and Tad turned aside to discuss mutual friends and CJ turned back to her presentation. Everything was in place. If she'd paid closer attention to her notes then she would have realized that P.T. Xtreme Sports was owned by Tad Randolph.

Normally, her secretary Marcia would have taken care of notifying her of such details. But Rae-Anne had been lucky to find the file on the company before they'd had to come down to the conference room.

She missed Marcia. They'd worked together for four years like a well-oiled machine until Marcia had fallen in love with Stuart Mann and married him. The couple had decided to start a family, which left CJ without Marcia's presence in the office. Not that she begrudged Marcia her family, she just wished they'd had more time to train this temp.

"You nervous?" Rae-Anne asked when Tad's other executives filled the conference room.

"I shouldn't be. This is routine." Sure, it's every day the boy you had a girlhood crush on was the key to an important account…and your promotion.

"Then why are you?" Rae-Anne asked.

"That's the million dollar question, Rae-Anne. Thanks for helping me set up. You can go back to the office now."

''No problem. Good luck, CJ.''

''I need more than luck,'' CJ said. She needed a miracle, but her life had been short on those.

Taking a deep breath, she squared her shoulders and began her presentation. She avoided meeting Tad's gaze. And spoke with all the confidence she'd cultivated since she'd left that small town she'd grown up in, and honed since Marcus had left her.

It would be a lot easier to deal with Tad's reappearance in her life if he weren't so damned attractive.

Remember what he said about you and how it felt to realize you'd put your trust in someone who was so superficial. Remember that Tad wasn't the only one to teach you that lesson. Marcus did as well.

How many times did she have to be hurt before she'd finally learned?

Her career had never let her down. Advertising was safer and required no heartache.

But there was a part of her—Cathy Jane—that wondered what it'd be like to kiss Tad Randolph, high school superstar. A little experiment to see if all the hype that had surrounded Tad during high school had been accurate.

She was no longer the girl with the baggy clothes and frizzy hair. She was a sophisticated city girl who knew how to make men take notice of her and wasn't afraid of their attention. At least in the boardroom she knew how to do it.

Life couldn't get much better, CJ thought. Once she started talking her confidence returned and she realized that even if Tad recognized her it wasn't the end of the world.

"I know you had a long-standing relationship with Tollerson but together we can take P.T. Xtreme Sports to the next level," she said.

"Very impressive. We'll be making our decision at the end of the week," Tad said, wrapping up her presentation.

He had a few words with Butch as CJ cleaned up her presentation boards. Not bad, she thought. She'd made it through the presentation and unless she'd missed her guess, P.T. Xtreme Sports was going to be the newest account in her impressive portfolio.

"Great job, CJ," Butch said.

"Thanks, Butch."

Butch walked out of the room and CJ felt like doing the Snoopy dance of joy.

Slowly the conference room emptied leaving only herself and Tad. Why was he still here?

Nervously, she tugged at the hem of her suit jacket. "I'm really impressed with you, CJ Terrence."

"Thanks," she said. She should just clear the air, tell him they'd gone to high school together and then put it behind her.

He moved closer. There was something sensual in his eyes. Was he attracted to her? He quirked on eyebrow at her as she took a half step backwards.

"Am I scary?" he asked.

"No."

He smiled at her and closed the gap she'd just

opened with her retreat. She tried to reassure herself that he wasn't stalking her. If she wanted to she could back away and give herself more space. But she didn't want to. He smelled good. Closing her eyes she inhaled deeply.

He took her hand again rubbing his thumb over the back of her knuckles. ''Are you sure we haven't met before?''

Oh, God. Not again. Why hadn't she run when she had the chance?

What was she going to say? The truth was she didn't want him to ever look at her and picture the girl she'd been. But having an account manager that lied to you didn't exactly inspire confidence.

The rubbing motion of his thumb was sending shots of awareness up her arm. Her hand was tingling and if she wasn't so reluctant to have her past discovered she'd actually enjoy this time with him.

''Well…Ms. Terrence.''

''Well what, Mr. Randolph?'' she said pulling her hand away.

Time to take control and get the heck out of the conference room.

''CJ Terrence…CJ…Cathy Jane?'' Tad asked.

She was frozen. Unable to think of anything intelligent to say she just nodded.

''Cat Girl, I knew you looked familiar,'' Tad said smiling.

Cat Girl…that's what she'd called herself senior year. CJ wished for a time machine. She wouldn't travel to the future to see the marvels it held, or to the distant past to visit Regency England. She'd travel back to her first year of high school.

She'd find her old locker and destroy the box of HoHos she'd always kept there. Then she'd give her teenaged self a makeover, pointing out gently that baggy clothes didn't make her look slimmer and finally giving her teenaged self the one piece of advice no one else had given her but someone really should have—never call yourself *Cat Girl*.

Even if you meant it tongue-in-cheek, some day when you're almost thirty it will sound humiliating and not funny.

Alas, there was no time machine and she'd just have to muddle through this as best she could. Tad Randolph didn't own the only large sporting goods chain looking for representation, she could find another one. Of course, by then Paul Mitchum, another ad executive, would have beaten her to the punch and her career with Taylor, Banks and Markim would be down the drain. CJ wished that the floor would open up and swallow her.

"That was a long time ago," she said at last. "I'm not that person anymore."

"Why didn't you say something sooner?" he asked.

"Come on Tad, honestly would you want Cathy Jane from Auburndale to represent your company?"

"You're not that woman anymore," he said.

"No, I'm not," she said. She met his gaze. His gray-green eyes had always fascinated her. There was more reflected there now than intelligence and fierce will. Now she saw a man with life experience. A man who tempted her to forget what she'd learned about men and maybe risk her heart on the gamble that this guy would be the one who'd never leave.

"I've got to get back to work."

"I won't keep you."

She gathered her presentation case and walked out of the conference room without looking back.

"CJ?"

She glanced over her shoulder at him.

"Have dinner with me?" he asked.

"Oh, Tad. I can't."

"Why not? Come on, Cathy Jane, for old time's sake."

"It's CJ now."

She was tempted but knew that nothing good came from dwelling on the past. Besides, Tad had been the reason why she'd moved away from Auburndale. After she'd overheard him talking about her to his friends she'd realized that she needed to start over where no one knew her.

And Chicago had seemed the right place for that. Except she'd learned that running away meant nothing unless you changed, too. She'd been the same shy, awkward girl until Marcus had left and forced her to take stock of her life.

She didn't really know how to handle men one-to-one. She started to shake her head.

"I know you've changed but we were once friends and I'd like to take you to dinner."

She couldn't stop her smile. They had been friends. He'd been the only kid her age in the neighborhood that summer they'd both been twelve—popularity and weight hadn't mattered. They'd ridden their bikes all over the city and spent all their time together. She'd forgotten those days.

There was a part of Tad that was very dear to her. Not the teenaged boy who'd been more concerned about his image than her feelings, but the friend she'd had when she'd first moved to the ridiculously small town of Auburndale. "You're bigger than you used to be."

She blushed when she realized how ridiculous that sounded.

"Geez, thanks! Come on. Just one meal. What could it hurt?"

She knew she shouldn't but couldn't resist the temptation he represented. He'd been her secret teenage crush, and he'd never noticed her as a woman...until now. It was a fantasy and as long as she remembered that she should be fine. "Okay, one dinner but that's it. We're probably going to be working together and I don't want things to get weird."

"I like your confidence, Cat Girl."

"Uh, Tad?"

"Yes."

"Don't call me that anymore."

''What's going to happen if I do? I am stronger than you now.''

''I'm a third degree black belt in Tae Kwon Do.''

''No kidding. I practice that martial art too.''

This was creepy. She shouldn't have that much in common with him—the boy who'd broken her heart and made her doubt she'd be a mate to any man. ''I'd love to spar with you.''

''Call me Cat Girl again and I'll give you a chance. I don't want to talk about old times.''

''I don't either. I want a chance to get to know the new you.''

She tried to smile as she walked away because she knew that there wasn't much new to her. She still felt like the same awkward person she'd always been.

# Two

Tad guessed that CJ had been trying to put him in his place but as he watched her walk away, enjoying the sight of her curvy hips swaying with each step she took, he didn't mind.

Man had she changed since high school. He remembered the lonely little girl who'd made him feel like a hero when he'd bandaged her scrapes after she'd fallen off her bike. He remembered her as a sweet shy girl who'd been too smart for him in high school. He also remembered the girl who'd refused to talk to him after senior prom. He'd always wondered why she had cut him off.

But this woman in the conference room had been a sexy blend of intelligence, savvy and sass. Just what he liked in his women.

His mom had been bugging him to look up Cathy Jane since he'd moved to Chicago five years ago, but Tad had put her off. Kylie, his college girlfriend, had left him saying she didn't want to come in second to a sporting goods store just about the time he had moved to the Windy City. Tad had been kind of sour on women then. The last thing he'd wanted to do was catch up with the girl who'd given him the cold shoulder through the last two months of their acquaintance.

Of course, at the time his mom had been pressuring him to marry as well. Which was a common thing with her. But his business had been in that crucial make-it-or-break-it stage and the last thing he'd wanted was the kind of distraction women offered. And he hadn't been interested in marrying some hometown girl or any other girl for that matter.

Tad had shelved his dreams of wife and family and concentrated on making a success of P.T. Xtreme Sports instead. But his mother's health had been deteriorating in the five years since he'd moved to Chi-town and he knew she'd love to see him settled. In fact, she'd hinted rather baldly on the phone last night that she was the only woman in her circle of friends without grandchildren. And he was honest enough to admit he wanted a family.

He'd created a legacy and he wanted to be able to pass it on to his own kids. But finding the right woman wasn't easy. He wanted a woman who'd look up to him and need him.

Cathy Jane would have fit that bill, but he wasn't

sure CJ did. She'd changed. He remembered long curly brown hair that he'd always tried to accidentally touch. God, it had been incredibly soft. Her auburn tinted tresses had been tucked up today. Was her hair still that soft, he wondered.

Her eyes had thrown him as well. She'd always had the biggest brown eyes behind her horn-rims. She looked good with blue eyes and if he'd never known her as Cathy Jane he might even prefer the blue. But he had known Cathy Jane. Why had she felt the need to change so much?

A small leather wallet was lying on the end of the table. He'd give it to one of the secretaries on his way out. He picked it up and it opened. Staring up at him from a typical DMV photo was Catherine Jane Terrence.

He skimmed her address. Her condo was only a few blocks from his. All this time they'd practically been neighbors and never run into each other. Tad was honest enough to admit he wouldn't have recognized her as his old childhood pal without hearing her name.

Whistling under his breath he left the conference room. A pretty brunette receptionist smiled up at him as he approached. He smiled back at her. "Can you direct me to Ms. Terrence's office?"

She gestured toward the left. Bangles rattled on her wrist. "Down the hall, third door on the left."

"Thank you."

He paused outside her doorway. He could hear CJ talking to her secretary. It didn't sound like CJ was having a great day. Frustration underlined each of her words. He was beginning to think that CJ worked too hard. It wasn't even lunchtime—way too early to be stressed out.

He rapped on the door frame. Both women looked up. CJ's secretary was a middle-aged woman with graying black hair and a few wrinkles. Both women wore identical expressions of frustration.

"Can I help you?" CJ asked.

"You left this in the conference room," Tad said. Oh, yeah he was a smooth talker with the women. Why was it that Cathy Jane made him feel like he was on his first date?

"Oh, thanks. You could have left it up front."

"Yes, I could have." This was going to be harder than he thought. Why was CJ so damned determined to keep things all business between them? Probably because, at this point, there was only business between them. Yet when they'd shook hands earlier in the conference room he'd felt something pass between them that had nothing to do with ad campaigns.

"I have a few questions to ask about your presentation, can you spare me five minutes?"

"Sure. Rae-Anne, why don't you go down the hall and ask Gina to show you around the office?"

Rae-Anne brushed past Tad muttering under her breath about bossy women and—while his Italian had never been good—he thought he heard her curse in that language.

"Your secretary is...different," he said at last.

"She's a temp. Today's her first day and we're still working out the kinks," CJ said. She leaned against the desk, fiddling with the clasp on her wallet. She tucked a strand of hair behind her ear. "What questions did you have?"

He didn't have any. He hadn't had a chance to review her presentation but he hadn't liked being dismissed. He'd learned a long time ago that the only way to achieve what he wanted was to take charge. He cleared his throat. "Just wanted to clarify a few details. We have an in-house production company for educational videos. We usually use them for our commercials as well."

"Come into my office. I want to make some notes," she said, leading him through the connecting door. Her office was a decent size with a large window overlooking Michigan Avenue. Her walls were decorated with awards and plaques of appreciation from companies.

The article Butch had referred to earlier was framed and hanging on the wall. CJ's picture was cool and confident. She hardly resembled Cathy Jane—the girl he'd known. But even then he'd known she'd go on to do great things. She'd been smart and shy but very focused on getting out of Auburndale.

"That shouldn't be a problem. When you make your decision, I'll get a contact name from you and talk to the head of the department."

"I'll do that," he said, leaning back in the leather guest chair. Her office was subtle and relaxing but also spoke of success. He felt a twinge of pride at how far she'd come from the girl she'd been. Despite the way things had ended between them, he'd always thought of her fondly.

"I can't believe you own a sporting goods store," she said.

"You're not the only one. I started college prelaw."

"You look sporty," she said, then rolled her eyes.

He didn't remember her being this funny. But then she'd always been so uncomfortable around him. His friends had teased him about spending so much time with a chubby brainiac. But deep down, he'd always liked Cathy Jane.

"Believe it or not, I am capable of intelligent conversation," she said.

He smiled. She'd always been one of the smartest people he knew. "You're the first person to call me sporty."

"I know you were an athlete in high school. Is that how you got into the business?"

"During college I started to work out more and tried some things I'd always wanted to."

"Like?"

"Mountain biking, rafting, some rock climbing."

"Do you still do all that?" she asked.

He nodded. "I was in Moab, Utah last week."

"You've changed so much," she said.

"So have you, Cathy Jane."

"I'm CJ, now, Tad. Some days it doesn't seem I've changed all that much," she said.

"Good. I always liked the girl you were."

"Is that why you told your friends I paid you to spend time with me?"

Tad hardly remembered the boy he had been until she'd said those words. He'd been more concerned with how he looked to his friends in those days than hurting Cathy Jane's feelings. Honestly, though he'd never known she'd overheard his remarks.

He was embarrassed by them now. No wonder she'd never talked to him after senior prom. "Hey, I was young and stupid."

"Yeah, so was I," she said.

"Does this mean you don't have a crush on me anymore?" he asked, cursing himself for not keeping quiet. Because a crush was the only thing that had explained her behavior back then.

CJ sank back in her chair unsure what to say next. She knew she should have run when she first had a glimpse of Tad Randolph. But his warm gray-green eyes had convinced her to stay before he'd even recognized their past connection. And she'd never had good instincts when it came to men.

When they'd been in high school she'd idolized Tad. She'd spent hours writing his name in her notebooks and dreaming of them together. But now, as a mature woman she understood things that never would have entered her mind then—like relationships were complex and needed both people to be interested.

Though Tad's comments had hurt, a part of her had

needed to hear what he really thought of her. It had given her the courage to break free from the familiar and start over. College had taught her more lessons and Marcus had finished her education when he'd left.

Tad leaned forward in his chair. Bracing his elbows on his knees and watching her with an intensity that made her breathless. She shivered under the impact. What was he thinking?

"Tad…" She stood and paced to the window. How could she explain to him that maybe she'd needed to hear the truth about herself. That his comments, though hurtful at the time, had made her realize that she needed to be strong inside. She needed to get away from her comfort zone and try the things she'd always secretly dreamed of.

She heard him stand but didn't turn. Maybe he was leaving. But then she felt his presence behind her. He patted her awkwardly on the shoulder.

"Sorry I said it that way," he said. His hand slid down her back lingering at the curve of her waist.

His touch rattled her senses and for a minute she wasn't sure what he'd said.

She wrinkled her nose, wishing again that Marcia still worked for her. Her old secretary would have interrupted by now and sent Tad on his way. "I hoped it wouldn't come up."

"I had no right to ask it," he said.

"I guess you did. There's no easy way to say this. I think I'd built you into someone you really weren't," she said.

''What kind of guy?'' he asked.

''The kind that looked past the outer shell of who I was and saw me as something more,'' she said. He'd been someone she could debate the merits of Voltaire versus Molière. He'd been someone who understood that sometimes it was easier to be smart than to socialize. He'd been a safe haven from the other popular boys who teased her endlessly.

He cupped her face and shivers of awareness spread down her body. He had always had that effect on her senses. The first time it had happened in the advanced biology lab she'd nearly freaked out. It still shook her.

''Would it help at all to know that I regretted the words as soon as they left my mouth?''

''*Yeah, right.* You always did have a touch of the blarney in you.'' It was nice of Tad to try to reassure her. Her reservations about men had started long before she'd met Tad and continued long after she'd left Auburndale.

He shrugged and let his hand drop. ''I only wish I'd had the maturity to make that moment right.''

''Well, you were responsible for my leaving town and making the life I've made. So maybe I should thank you.''

''I knew you went to Northwestern. Was it what you expected?'' he asked.

''No,'' she said. But it had definitely helped her grow up and had cemented her decision to make her career her life.

"You'll have to tell me about it," he said. He crossed back to the guest chair.

"Now?" she asked, walking back to her desk. She wasn't going to tell him a thing about that time in her life or Marcus Fielding.

He shook his head. "I have to get back to work."

"Of course. You rattled me, Tad."

"I know," he said, wriggling his eyebrows. "I have a feeling not many do that, Miss Top Thirty."

"You've got that right. Next time we meet I'm going to be on my toes." Or at least give the impression she was. She knew herself well enough to know that Tad was always going to knock her a little off balance.

It didn't seem fair that the one guy who had that ability should be the only thing standing between her and the realization of her career goals.

"I'd rather you weren't," he said.

She smoothed her skirt and cocked her head to one side. "That's what all the men say."

"Do they?" he asked.

"You know they do. Guys don't like smart women," she said, teasing him.

"Only dumb guys don't like smart women," he said with a cocky grin.

She'd forgotten what it was like to spar with a man. The men she'd dated lately tended to be as career focused as she was. "You never were dumb. Though, I may have to revise my opinion."

"Why?" He took a step toward her.

Although she realized she never should have started

this, she wouldn't back down now. "You look like a jock."

He tucked his hands into his pockets and canted his hips to one side. Her breath caught in her chest. His pose was blatantly masculine and unexpected. He sounded like her childhood friend but there was an aura of sexuality and macho self-confidence the Tad she'd known had never used around her.

"I own a sporting goods company. I am a jock."

"That's what I was afraid of," she said, trying to force him back into that comfortable mold he'd previously inhabited in her mind.

He raised one eyebrow at her in question and cocked his head at her.

"I'm trying to think of a way to put this delicately…"

"You don't have to mince words with me," he said, taking another step toward her.

She edged back stopping only when her desk blocked her retreat. "I'm just afraid that buff body of yours may have cost you a bit of the gray matter."

"You think I'm buff, Cathy Jane?"

She blushed as she realized she did. It was never a good idea to fall into lust with your client. She cleared her throat. "Please don't call me that."

Taking his hands from his pockets, he ran one finger down the side of her face. "Why not?"

"Because I'm not that girl anymore," she said.

He leaned closer to her. His minty breath brushing

her face with each word he spoke. "You're so much more than you used to be, Cathy Jane."

Pivoting on his heel he walked out the door. CJ put her hand over her racing heart and knew she'd just met more than her match. She would have to avoid spending any time alone with him.

Saturday dawned bright and chilly. Tad left his condo and ran along the shore of Lake Michigan. CJ had been ducking his calls all week and frankly he was tired of it. He'd let her have her space but that was all about to end. He was a man of action and winning games was something he'd become accustomed to.

The rhythm of his exercise cleared his mind and soon he was analyzing Cathy Jane. He hadn't realized she'd heard his comments to Bart all those years ago. He'd never meant for her to be hurt and he'd actually gone on to defend her. But guys like Bart never really understood women.

Tad realized he didn't understand them either. Kylie had wanted a rich husband and Tad had worked his butt off to make his dreams of a sporting goods store come true. But Kylie hadn't been satisfied with that. As he worked to build his business, she'd complained that she didn't want a man who worked all the time.

What kind of a mate would CJ be? She was successful in her own right and wouldn't need a man's money to support her. But would she want a man to share her life?

He'd talked to his mom again this morning, casually mentioning that he'd run into Cathy Jane. His mom had asked about CJ and her sister Marnie.

''Nice girls, nice family,'' his mom had said, and he knew what she'd meant. The kind of girl she wished he'd marry. He'd hung up without saying anymore to his mom about CJ. But she'd planted a seed in his head.

Would CJ be willing to marry him? They were both nearing thirty and their careers were on track.

He'd got her to agree to dinner but little else. She'd hedged and had her secretary send regrets twice. But Tad was used to hard work.

He ran his usual five miles, but altered his route so that he jogged by CJ's building on his way home. He'd always had a photographic memory and the image of her address on her driver's license was etched in his mind. Could he drop by unannounced? He slowed as he approached her building.

Two women were struggling with a Christmas tree. He slowed his pace. He thought it was CJ and an older woman. He still wasn't used to seeing her with auburn hair. In his mind she had thick ebony hair. She looked cute with her knit cap and matching muffler around her neck. Her companion looked like her secretary.

He slowed to a walk to let his breathing slow and even out and then approached her. All he could make out was her long black wool jacket, legs encased in faded denim and a pair of boots that would have done any one in Auburndale proud.

"Rae-Anne, can you lift your end a little higher?" CJ asked. The two women juggled the tree without much success. The six-foot blue spruce was a nice tree—not unlike the one that he'd ordered for his condo. For someone who'd changed so much, they still had a lot in common.

"*Madon'*. I'm trying. I'm not as strong as I used to be," Rae-Anne said.

"Let's set it down for a second," CJ said, bending at the waist to set the trunk on the snow-dusted ground. Her coat slid up and Tad was treated to the full curves of her backside. His fingers tingled with the need to reach out and caress her.

Instincts older than time had his hand lifting before he could stop himself. Her buttocks looked firm and full, but he'd learned the hard way that women didn't appreciate a man reaching out and grabbing something he liked. She straightened, still holding the tree up.

"Can I help?" Tad asked, reaching around CJ to take the trunk of the tree from her.

CJ glanced over her shoulder at him. Her breath brushed across his cheek and he inhaled sharply. The scent that was uniquely CJ assailed him. He was surprised at its familiarity. It reminded him of home and of memories best forgotten.

"What are you doing here?"

"I live up the street," he said, gesturing to his building. "Let me carry the tree up for you."

"Thanks, but we've got it," CJ said, brushing his arm aside. He refused to let her budge his arm.

She glared up at him but he knew she wouldn't make an issue of it in front of her secretary. "We don't need your help."

"*Merda,* I do," Rae-Anne said. She put her hand over her heart and sighed loudly. "Some of us aren't as young as we used to be. And I just stopped by to drop off the Monday files. I finally figured out your last secretary's system."

CJ bit her lower lip, unsure. He knew her well enough to know that she didn't like to give ground. He sometimes wondered, if he hadn't let her beat him in arm wrestling when they'd been twelve, if they'd have even been friends.

Tad took control, grabbing the tree and hefting it with one hand. "I got the tree."

"Very impressive. Do the girls usually swoon when you do this?"

"You're my first, CJ," he said.

"I'm impressed. Are you sure you won't drop it?"

Always the smart-ass, when they'd been teenagers she'd teased him about his choice of girlfriends. He'd forgotten that there'd always seemed to be two different Cathy Janes. The one at school who kept her head down and her nose in a book and the one at home who sassed him. He wondered what she'd do if he kissed her. Her lips were full and he was tempted more than he should be. His plan for a wife was simple and straightforward—filling a void in his life. "I can handle one tree, CJ."

"Of course, you can," Rae-Anne said. "You're not a middle-aged woman."

"Kind of you to notice," Tad said, smiling at the other woman.

"Think nothing of it," Rae-Anne said. "I believe in giving credit where it's due."

"So do I. Machismo isn't something that requires praise, Rae-Anne," CJ said.

"Machismo?" he asked. A man had to have a strong ego around CJ. Unlike Kylie who'd always flattered him...until she'd walked out the door with one of his competitors.

CJ tilted her head to the side and studied him. He couldn't help it. He flexed his abs and stood a little taller. Her gaze moved over him and his blood flowed heavier. He shifted his legs trying to keep her from noticing his stirring erection through the fabric of his sweatpants. "Overabundance of testosterone sound better?"

Oh, yeah, he was going to kiss that smart mouth. To hell with her Christmas tree. "Gallant rescue sounds good to me."

"You always did have a big head."

"You always were a bit of a pain."

"Then why are you here?" she asked.

Because she was the one woman he'd never been able to forget. No matter how many beautiful, intelligent women he'd dated, CJ had always lingered in the back of his mind. "I'm a glutton for punishment."

"Follow me. I'm on the twelfth floor. We have to use the service elevator," CJ said.

"I'm yours to command."

"As if," she said and climbed the stairs to the building.

Rae-Anne and CJ held the doors open for Tad, and in a short time they were standing in CJ's apartment.

"Where's your tree stand?" he asked.

"I can do that. I don't want to take up too much of your time."

"I don't mind."

"Really that's okay."

"You can't do it on your own," he said.

"Rae-Anne is going to help me, right?" she asked.

Rae-Anne had a pile of file folders in her arms and didn't really look like she'd expected to decorate a tree.

"Do you want me to help?" Rae-Anne asked. "My mother used to say many hands make light work."

Tad winked at her, sensing he had found an ally in his pursuit of CJ. And he just realized it was a pursuit and nothing less than complete surrender of the saucy redhead would suit him.

# Three

CJ had had enough interaction for the day. Saturdays were normally her favorite. She wanted Rae-Anne to go home and Tad to disappear back into the fabric of the past so that she could once again have control of her life. She'd make herself a nice cup of herbal tea and then climb onto the counter and pull down the box of HoHos she had stored above the refrigerator.

They were for emergency use only and after this day she knew she needed the sweet bliss that only consuming a box of chocolate cream-filled cakes could bring.

She'd talked to Rae-Anne last night and they'd discussed Rae-Anne bringing over the Monday files so they could have a head start on the week. But then

Rae-Anne had called to say she'd be late and CJ had decided to go and get her Christmas tree. Bad idea. She should have gone into the office instead. Nothing was the same with Rae-Anne as it had been with Marcia.

But Tad was a different matter entirely. The purely masculine look in his eyes told her that he was interested in doing more than renewing old friendships and frankly, that made her nervous.

She was glad that Rae-Anne was here because she didn't want to be alone with Tad.

Her weary soul said no more guys with buff bodies and yet she'd always been drawn to them. Marcus had been a marathon runner who'd spent hours in the gym. Even her dad had been a high school football coach.

"I'll make the coffee," she suddenly blurted.

And for some reason being around Tad seemed to reduce her normally quick tongue to banal small talk. More and more she was slipping back into the old Cathy Jane, joke of Auburndale high school.

"I'll make it," Rae-Anne said.

"No offense, Rae-Anne, but you have yet to make a pot of coffee that anyone would drink."

Rae-Anne threw back her head and laughed. "*Madon',* this woman thing is making me crazy."

"What woman thing?" Tad asked.

"You wouldn't believe me if I told you," Rae-Anne said. Turning to a battered box she pulled out a tangled mess of Christmas lights.

"We've got our work cut out, my friend."

"I think I can handle it."

CJ left them to sort out the lights telling herself there was nothing wrong with escaping to the kitchen. Not long ago she'd vowed to never let a man make her cower again and here she was hiding out in her kitchen. She boiled water in her teakettle and made coffee in her French press. She had a box of cookies in the cupboard and she arranged them on a Christmas plate from the set her mother had given her the year before she'd died.

There was a part of CJ that really hated the holidays. Marcus had broken up with her on Christmas Eve five years ago and he'd changed something inside her when he left.

She'd hoped to marry him and become his wife. She'd had visions of a shared future where they had their own small ad agency and they worked together. But Marcus had needed something else in a wife. He'd been using her to get a promotion and once he had obtained it, he'd dumped her for the right woman. A corporate wife who'd put her husband first instead of her career.

Her father had run off just after Thanksgiving the year she was eleven with an eighteen-year-old cheerleader. And her mom had been diagnosed with cancer two days after Christmas when CJ was nineteen. So, the holidays always represented not just joy in a season of giving, but also sadness and a sense of loss at what could never be again.

"Rae-Anne sent me to help you."

CJ made a mental note to talk to Rae-Anne. That woman was entirely too bossy for her own good. ''I think I can handle coffee and a plate of cookies.''

Tad stepped into her ''step-saver'' kitchen and CJ backed up a pace.

''Did I suddenly develop some communicable disease?'' he asked.

She flushed. ''No, why?''

''Because you keep dancing away from me. What's up, Cathy Jane?''

She forced herself to stand her ground when Tad came closer to her. It wasn't that she was afraid of him. It was her reactions that made her leery. Not even Marcus who she'd contemplated marrying had made her skin tingle, her pulse pound and her body ache the way Tad did.

''Nothing.''

He reached out and caressed her face. Drew his large callused forefinger down the side of her cheek. His wizard green eyes watched her carefully and she struggled to keep any sign of what she was feeling from her face. Marcus had taught her that men wouldn't hesitate to use a woman's body against her.

''I know you better than that.''

She shivered again as he took his hand from her face and turned to the plate of cookies. God, she hoped he didn't really know her. Didn't realize that her feminine instincts were stronger than her control. And that at this moment she wanted nothing more than to order

Rae-Anne from the condo and beg Tad to touch her once again.

"Not anymore, you don't," she said quietly. The only element in her favor was that Tad was a stranger.

"The other day in your office you weren't like this."

"Well, we were in my office. You were a client, not a guy in clinging sweatpants lifting heavy things with one hand."

"Did I impress you?" he asked, pivoting back toward her, pinning her between the kitchen cabinet and him.

She had to tilt her head back to meet his gaze and when she did, she wished she'd hadn't. There was a heat there that mirrored the longing in her soul. Nervously she licked her lips. His eyes tracked the movement and he leaned the tiniest bit toward her before stopping.

"Do you want to?" she asked.

"Hell, yeah."

Her blood ran heavier in her veins and she knew that what she wanted—really wanted—was for him to notice her as a woman. No matter how dangerous that attraction would be, she wanted it.

But she hadn't lost her mind. This new Tad was too big. Too "large and in charge" as her ten-year-old niece, Courtney would say.

"I'm not in the ego-building business."

"Cathy Jane, this has nothing to do with ego," he

said. He settled his hands on her hips and drew her closer to him.

''Tad, I really don't think...''

''That's right, don't think.''

He lowered his head toward hers. Her hands rose to his shoulders and instead of doing the prudent thing and pushing him away, she kneaded his shoulders, leaned up on tiptoe and met his hungry mouth with her own. Oh, my God, she thought, Tad Randolph is kissing me.

Tad wouldn't have guessed that her mouth would taste so sweet. She was shy and hesitant and he coaxed her gently into opening her mouth wider and letting him explore her hidden secrets. Ah, yes, this was what he'd been searching for.

She didn't lie passively in his embrace. But she didn't take charge either as he'd expected her to do. At work she was a modern-day Amazon but in his arms he realized there was still a lot of the shy, sweet girl he used to know.

Her touches were tentative on his shoulders and back. Her mouth under his was soft. Her curves were pliant against him. He pulled her more fully into his body and held her for a minute. His mouth pressed against hers in the chaste embrace she seemed to need.

He lifted his head and dropped light kisses on her cheeks and forehead. Her eyes were the remembered dark brown today instead of the blue-green contacts she'd worn that day in her office. She watched him warily and he wanted to reassure her. To promise her that he didn't want to hurt her only show her a passion that he suspected would be Heaven on earth.

"Relax, CJ, let me in. I promise it'll feel good."

"We have to work together," she said.

"That sounds like an excuse."

"It is. God, it really is. But you aren't what I expected, Tad. And I have no idea how to handle this," she said. Her voice rasped over his aroused senses with the same impact as silk over skin.

He didn't have words to reassure her. Wasn't sure that this was a good idea from his vantage point either but he knew there was no way he was leaving the kitchen having only shared one kiss.

"Cathy Jane, you slay me," he said and lowered his mouth once again to hers. This time he took her lower lip between his teeth and suckled. He was so tight and full and needed her more than he'd ever admit.

He slid his hands down her torso, skimming the full curves of her breasts and spanning her waist. He bent his knee and thrust his leg between hers. She grasped his shoulders and her mouth opened with a soft sound.

Holding her head in his hands, he tilted her face back and took her mouth the way he wanted to take her. Fast, hard, deep and so thoroughly that she'd never again touch her lips and not think of him.

She smelled of a sweet floral scent that was wholly feminine. And felt like pure fire in his arms. He slid his hands down her back and around the curve of her waist. Moaning in the back of her throat, she kneaded his shoulders. He thrust his tongue deeper in her mouth. Until she was clutching at his shoulders and returning his embrace fully.

There was something challenging about the woman CJ had become. Something in her eyes and walk that told all men—especially Tad—that she wasn't an easy woman to seduce. But he'd always been a determined man.

He traced the line of her spine down her back to the full curves of her buttocks. Damn, her butt felt as good in his hands as he'd known it would. He wanted to deepen the caress. Her jeans molded to her curves and he couldn't resist tracing the center seam between her legs. She moaned again, scraping the edge of her fingernail around the neckband of his sweatshirt. His arousal grew heavier. Every nerve ending felt hyper-sensitive.

He slid his hands back up her body. She was so womanly. He needed to touch more of her and the only way to do that was to slip his hands under her shirt. She made one of those soft sweet sounds he was becoming addicted to.

He caressed her back and plundered her mouth. Content for now to have her in his arms and be able to taste this small part of her. A part of him knew that he wouldn't be able to stop if he let things continue much longer.

He peppered her face with a few small kisses and slowly slid his hands out from under her shirt. He continued to hold her in his embrace until his pulse stopped racing. His erection was still heavy between his legs but he was old enough to know he wasn't going to die from it.

He stepped back after a minute. CJ fingered her lips with tentative fingers and watched him as if unsure what he wanted from her. He thrust his fingers through his hair and wondered when his simple plan to marry her had become so complicated.

"Um…I better bring the coffee out to Rae-Anne."

She tried to skirt around him but he stopped her by blocking her path. He knew it was childish but there was something about CJ that made him react from the gut instead of from the head.

"This isn't over," he said. He didn't know why she was running but realized that life had changed this woman more than he'd realized.

Crossing her arms over her chest she glared up at him. He felt like a big mean bully and wanted to pull her back into his arms and kiss away her irritation.

"Yes, it is."

"Why?" he asked, not willing to let the subject drop. "It can't be because of one comment in high school."

"It's not."

He waited but she didn't say anything else.

She sighed and then looked at the floor. Finally in a small voice she said, "I don't have affairs."

Now we're getting somewhere. "Why not?"

"Life is easier that way."

Life was going to be damned hard for him until he had her in his bed, writhing under him. "I'm not going away."

"You will."

Her confidence threw him. She'd been the one to leave him all those years ago. "Don't count on it, Cathy Jane. I have plans for you."

"Business plans, I know."

"I'm going to marry you," he said, surprising himself. But the words sounded right in his soul. She was exactly the kind of woman he'd been unconsciously searching for. He'd been thinking of marriage a lot lately.

He wanted her to be his wife. He wanted her to be the mother of his children. He wanted her in his bed and it had nothing to do with the fact that his parents wanted him to give them grandkids.

"What?"

Having blurted out his announcement, he had no choice but to keep going. Damn, this is what happened when he let his groin do the thinking. He should have eased into his announcement but she'd been backing away and he'd wanted to put his mark on her. To claim her as his even though he didn't have the right.

"You heard me. I've analyzed the facts and I think we'd be very successful together as a married couple."

And he did believe that. He'd tried love with Kylie and ended up frustrated and alone. Marriages, the really successful ones he'd noticed, were based on common likes, similar backgrounds and physical compatibility.

CJ thought maybe she'd stepped into one of those alternate realities like they had on *Star Trek: The Next Generation* sometimes—like the one where Tasha Yarr was really alive and married to a Romulan. Tad watched her with that mix of determination and intelligence that she'd come to recognize meant he wasn't backing down.

She was still trying to assimilate all the feelings from him kissing her. It had been a high school dream and something she'd imagined a million times. But the reality had been so much more. Now she knew his taste, his touch. The way his hands felt on her face. And the way he'd closed his eyes just halfway as they'd pulled apart. Dammit. She didn't want to think about the kiss.

Instead she jumped on the one subject that was a powerful distraction. Marriage.

''Are you nuts?''

''No. I'm serious about this.''

''We don't know each other,'' she said. And there was a part of her that was really glad he didn't know her. There were certain secrets she wasn't going to share with anyone—especially a man.

''Sure we do. Plus we have a lot in common.''

''Name one thing.''

''We're from the same small town.''

"That barely counts. And we don't live there anymore. Name something else."

"We both chose the same type of Christmas tree."

"Tad, have you fallen on your head lately? You don't marry someone because they like the same things as you do."

"Just think about how peaceful our Christmases will be."

"There's more to life than Christmas."

"I know. We also live only a few blocks apart and work in the same area of town."

"So do hundreds of other people. That hardly means we're meant to be."

"Yeah, but hundreds of other guys haven't kissed you."

"You hadn't either until today, so I don't see what that has to do with anything."

"Maybe you are the one woman I've never been able to forget, Cathy Jane," he said, quietly.

"Is that true?" she asked. When he called her Cathy Jane it made her feel cherished. Not like a corporate warrior who'd carved a place for herself in the world, but like a woman who'd found a special spot with the right man.

She watched those wizard eyes of his carefully. They revealed no emotion to her and she sensed that he was trying to decide if pretending he was in love with her despite the time that had passed between them would win her. But she'd been lied to by men her entire life and she'd learned long ago not to believe what they said.

"Forget I asked," she said. She'd learned some tough lessons about men. You'd think she'd have enough smarts to stop asking them questions like that.

"I won't forget you asked. I want you to say yes, CJ...."

"But you can't admit that I've been on your mind. I'm not asking you to confess undying love."

"Good. Love is such an indefinable thing."

"It's not a thing, it's an emotion. Do you have those?"

"Sure, I do."

"Just not for me?" she asked.

He gave her an aggrieved look. What had happened to Tad in his past relationships? Something in his tone told her that he was hiding an important detail from her. "We don't really know each other."

"My point exactly," she said. Marriage was... scary. She didn't know that she'd ever be able to risk her heart on happily ever after since every time she'd counted on that, she'd lost.

"Which is why our marriage will work."

"How do you know this? Did you try it once before and fail?"

"No. I've never made it to the church."

He must have gotten close. She wanted to find out more about his past relationship but didn't want to probe too deeply. "Then how can you be so sure?"

"I watched a friend of mine get torn apart in the name of love."

There was a fierceness about him that told her that he did experience deep emotion. For a minute she mourned the fact that she wasn't the person inspiring that emotion in him. But she'd looked in the mirror. She knew her limits.

She was the meat and potatoes kind of girl. A solid meal that would keep you alive. She wasn't the fancy French pastry that everyone craved. It was time she stopped forgetting it.

"I don't plan to ever marry," she said at last. She wasn't settling in her personal life and fully expected to remain single because she was realistic enough to realize no man could give her everything she wanted from him.

"Cathy Jane, forget those dreams you have of a white knight. We can have a nice, comfortable life together."

Screw you, she thought. What was she a pair of bedroom slippers? Sure she knew that she didn't exactly have it going on when it came to being a sexy goddess but that didn't mean she was comfortable.

"No. Thanks."

"No to what?" he asked as she pushed past him and gathered napkins and paper plates.

"To marriage," she said under her breath.

"I haven't asked you yet."

Stunned she pivoted to face him. He watched her

with a calm implacability that made her want to scream. "You are so frustrating."

He gave her a half smile that she was sure he intended to lighten the mood. But nothing could. She'd only seriously considered marrying two men in her life. Tad when she'd been eighteen, which had been pure fantasy.

And then Marcus when she'd been twenty-three, which had been harsh reality. Now Tad was here asking her to marry him and she wanted to say yes but she couldn't...wouldn't. She wasn't risking her heart and soul for another man. No matter how attractive he was or how sincere his offer of forever sounded.

"So are you."

Picking up the cookie platter she hurried out into the living room. Rae-Anne was standing back staring at the tree. For a moment there was a look on her face that gave CJ pause. Her secretary had an aura of sadness around her.

"You okay, Rae-Anne?"

Slowly Rae-Anne turned to face CJ. "Yeah."

"Do you want to talk about it?" CJ asked.

"Hell, no."

CJ set down the cookie tray and Tad was right behind her with the coffee. Her living room was spacious and had a nice grouping of a sofa and a couple of chairs. Rae-Anne took one of the armchairs and Tad stood next to one of the other ones. So CJ sat on the sofa.

She focused on serving coffee and then relaxed

against the cushions. Tad didn't sit down, just propped one hip against the arm of the chair and watched her with that wizard's gaze of his.

She had the feeling he wanted to pursue the topic they'd been discussing in the kitchen. He was going to be disappointed because she wasn't ever going to be alone with him again. And the topic of marriage was *not* going to come up if she had any say so.

"What were you two talking about?" Rae-Anne asked.

"Our marriage," Tad said around a bite of cookie.

"I didn't realize you two were serious. When will the blessed event take place?" Rae-Anne asked.

"When hell freezes over," CJ said.

# Four

**T**ad threw his head back and laughed. Despite CJ's homey living room with the Christmas tree, a part of him wondered if she was going to be worth the battle. He'd lost at love before even though he hadn't told CJ the details. Losing Kylie had changed him. It had made him realize that life was more than winning and that sometimes a loss could cut deep.

She crossed the room to the stereo and put on a CD that played Christmas tunes. But CJ had so much sass and spunk—way more than he remembered Cathy Jane having. He couldn't wait to get her into bed. He had a feeling this glimpse of the real CJ was one not many people saw. "It's certainly cold enough to freeze hell today."

"I'm not kidding," she said, taking a large sip of her coffee. There was a hint of vulnerability in her eyes that he knew she'd regret revealing. There was so much more to his Catwoman than he expected. She'd always been complicated, he just hadn't been mature enough to appreciate her.

He waited until she swallowed then made sure she was watching him. "Good. I like a challenge."

"Is that all this is? A game?" CJ asked.

It was more than a game and more than he wanted to admit to himself. He didn't know why but she'd become important to his future.

The CJ he'd kissed in the kitchen was gone and in her place was the modern-day amazon he'd first encountered in CJ's office. The hint of vulnerability he'd glimpsed in her was now carefully concealed. Would the real Catherine Jane please step forward? "Would you play with me if it was?"

"No, Tad. Marriage is a sacred bond," CJ said.

"Not everyone thinks of it that way," he said, gently. Kylie certainly hadn't. She'd thought of it as a business transaction and the more money he'd brought to the table the more viable a husband candidate he'd been. Only at the time he hadn't realized it. Wouldn't even listen to Pierce when he'd tried to warn him that Kylie was only with Tad because of his bank account.

Pierce was his partner and best friend, a paraplegic who'd endured a lot in the name of love.

"Women do. Right, Rae-Anne?"

"I'm not the best one to ask about this," Rae-Anne said, staring down into her coffee cup.

Tad watched the older woman. There was no ring on her finger. But that didn't mean anything.

"Divorced?" CJ asked.

"I never had the time for marriage."

"Gay?" Tad asked.

"No. I just never took the time to settle down," Rae-Anne said.

"Do you regret that?" Tad asked her.

"Recently, I've started to. But my job used to be the most important thing in my life."

"Well, my job still is. And I'm not going to give it up for some guy," CJ said, standing up and walking toward the bank of glass windows that provided a clear view of Lake Michigan.

Tad set his coffee cup down and walked up behind her. Placing his hands on her shoulders he tugged her back against his chest. Damn but this woman felt right in his arms. "I'm not just any guy."

She tilted her head back and looked up at him. "No, you're not."

He cupped her face in his hand. "Is that the problem then?"

"There is no problem. I'm just not the marrying kind."

"Why not marry Tad?" Rae-Anne asked.

CJ pulled away from him. Tad had forgotten the older woman's presence. He wished he and CJ were by themselves in her apartment. They communicated more honestly when he was touching her than at any other time. He was sure once he had her alone and in his arms, he could convince her to marry him.

"He's a pain in the butt," CJ said.

"Perhaps he just knows what he wants," Rae-Anne said.

Having the older woman as an ally was definitely going to be an advantage. But then maybe Rae-Anne had regrets that she couldn't go back and change. "Thanks, Rae-Anne."

"Why are you on his side?"

"I just don't want to see you end up like me."

"Is that a sin?"

"Some people think so," Rae-Anne said.

Rae-Anne's phone rang and she answered it. After a terse conversation, Rae-Anne disconnected the phone. "Some people just don't know when to leave well enough alone. Do you need anymore help from me?"

"No. Thanks for bringing by my files and for your help with the tree. I'll see you tomorrow afternoon with the rest of the staff for the tree decorating party."

Rae-Anne left and an awkward silence fell between them.

"What have you got against marriage?" Tad asked, propping one hip against the armchair. CJ's apartment was tastefully decorated in a feminine way. Lots of light colors and baskets for magazines. But he felt comfortable here. Something he'd never felt in any other place except his parents' home.

"I'm not willing to give up everything for a man."
She was staring down into her coffee cup.

"That sounds bitter," Tad said.

She shrugged and finally glanced up at him. "Not
bitter—realistic."

He left his perch on the chair and sat down next to
her. Leaning back, he placed his arm along the top of
the loveseat over her shoulders. She started and jerked
away from him. Sloshing coffee onto her hands.

She put the cup on the table and wiped her hands
on a napkin but didn't relax. Just sat there tensely
waiting for him to pounce. Gee, that made him feel
good. What had he done to make her believe he was
the enemy?

"In the kitchen you asked me about love. Anyone
who believes in love can't be totally against marriage."

She started gathering items on the coffee table as if
cleaning up the cookies and coffee cups were the most
important thing in the world.

"Aren't you going to answer me?" he asked.

She glanced over her shoulder at him and he regretted pushing her. He knew one of his greatest faults
was impatience.

"I'll admit I want to find someone to love me—not
just an image that I represent."

"Cathy Jane, you've always been in your own playing field."

"Don't say things like that. You don't mean them,"
she said.

But he did. And convincing her of it would take considerable effort. But then everything worth keeping in his life had taken hard work. Why should CJ be any different?

He thought about his best friend, Pierce, who'd lost the woman he loved when he'd lost the use of his legs. His friend's devastation in the aftermath of losing Karen had confirmed to Tad that he never wanted to feel that way. He'd learned that it didn't pay to let a woman close. Tad had vowed to never let himself be affected so deeply by any woman.

But even that warning wasn't enough to sway him from wanting CJ. She turned away from him and he had the first doubts that his plan for a simple marriage of convenience might not work.

"Come to dinner with me tonight and I'll prove that I'm the only man you want."

"I don't think so," she said, gathering the tray with emptied coffee cups and leftover cookies. She couldn't focus on Tad and his insane desire to have her as his wife. It didn't matter that she was tempted, hell more than tempted to be Mrs. Tad Randolph. All that mattered was that she'd found a way of living that worked for her and she wasn't willing to rock the boat for some buff blond guy.

"I'll help with that." Tad stood to take the tray from her but she turned away.

She didn't want to make this decision with her hormones and just those few minutes in his arms earlier told her that saying no to Tad was the only sane option. She'd learned at Marcus' hands that she was a slave to her body and heart. And she wasn't going to live through that again.

"No, thanks."

He blocked her path to the kitchen. Determination written in every line of his body. Dammit, she wished he were still the ninety-pound weakling he'd been when they were twelve. Then she'd have brushed right past him and outrun him. But now, he looked like he could take on Mt. Everest blindfolded and she felt like she'd be doing good to get through a thirty-minute yoga class.

"I'm not leaving until you agree to have dinner with me," he said, drawing one finger down the side of her face. He toyed with a tendril of hair at the back of her neck. Her hands trembled.

"Why'd you dye your hair?" he asked, leaning forward around the tray. He brushed his nose against her head and breathed deeply. "You smell good."

She was shaking now, the coffee cups clattering on their saucers. Tad took the tray from her and put it on the coffee table. "Answer me."

"What?" she asked, totally rattled. All she wanted was to grab his hand and take him down the rather short hallway to her bedroom. She wanted to push him back on the bed and have her way with him.

"Your new hair color, why?"

How could she explain to this very attractive man that being an average mousy-brown-haired woman wasn't what she wanted the world to see of her? He wouldn't be able to understand that physical image was the easiest thing to change and still the most important to her. It was one more facade between her and the rest of the world.

She shrugged, trying for nonchalance, which she was far from feeling. "I needed to make a clean break with the past."

"Was it really that bad?" he asked.

He was too close. She could smell the sweat that had dried on his body. She wanted to do what he'd done, lean in and breathe in his essence but she couldn't. One lungful of his scent wouldn't be enough.

She wanted to indulge all her senses with him. To forget all this talk and communicate in the most essential way men and women could. Except she knew such communication was the most dangerous of all. "No. It didn't fit with the new me."

"I like the new you," he said, brushing his lips against hers. "But, then, I liked the old you too."

It wasn't enough. That brief brush of lips. She stood on her toes and kissed him. She closed her eyes, held his head in her hands and tasted him. She thrust her tongue past the barrier of his lips and teeth. The flavor of coffee and cookies deluged her taste buds.

She tilted her head to the side, pulling back then returning again to his mouth. He kept his hands at his sides letting her control the embrace. Seeming to know that she needed a chance to be in charge. Or maybe he knew this was the key to her weakness. She backed away abruptly. When was she going to learn?

He licked his lips, crossing his arms over his chest. His eyes watched her and she didn't know what to do next. This situation was not her comfort zone. She wanted him out of her house. *Now*.

"It's been a long time since…"

"Me too," he said, rubbing his thumb over her lower lip.

She ached for him in the most primal way. Her breasts were full and heavy. Her nipples taut. If she leaned forward just an inch she'd be able to rub against his chest. That hard well-developed-buff-sports-guy chest of his that called to her like the HoHos in her kitchen cupboard. But she wasn't ready to surrender everything for him. "I'm not sleeping with you, Tad."

"I don't really want to sleep," he said blandly.

She couldn't help but smile. "Please, just let it go."

"I can't. You're going to be my wife, CJ. You know I don't say things that I don't mean."

"Stop it," she said, backing away from him. He did so say things he didn't mean. He'd been the one to promise her at age twelve that he'd always rescue her and then he'd hurt her.

The next condo she bought was going to have a huge labyrinth of rooms. In it she would be able to stand at one end of the maze and have to yell to be heard at the other.

In such a complex, a six-foot tall man couldn't dominate any one room. She could easily escape not only a person, but the feelings and memories they evoked. "You don't know the real me. I don't think *I* do."

"That might be true. But I'm not leaving until I do."

"Why?"

"Because I know you'll avoid me from now on unless we clear the air."

"Clear the air. Is that all you want to do with me?"

"Hell, no. I want to take you to bed and break down all the barriers you've put between us."

"Tad, go away."

"Why?"

"Because I'm not the girl you want."

"Yes, you are."

"Because I like the same Christmas tree you do."

He gave her a half smile that took her breath away. "No, because you're beautiful and sexy and you've haunted my dreams since the last time I saw you."

She took the tray and left the living room. She couldn't think when he said things like that. When he made her believe that forever and happily ever after might still exist. It was as if everything Marcus, her ex-lover and ex-boss, had taught her disappeared. But she knew better.

"I'm not your dream woman, Tad. I'm no man's."

No man's dream woman. The words echoed in his head and Tad realized he'd unintentionally hurt CJ. The woman he thought had no weaknesses had just revealed one. And it was a deep wound. He felt like he'd callously torn the scab off of it.

As badly as Kylie had hurt him when she'd left, Tad had never been bitter toward women. For one thing Pierce wouldn't let him. He'd said one sour apple didn't make the whole pie bad. And Pierce had been right. There had been other women since Kylie, but now Tad acknowledged that he'd kept them at arm's length. Something he wasn't going to be able to do with CJ.

He knew a gentleman would leave but he'd never held that title. He was a businessman and sports enthusiast. He'd been a farmer and a brainiac. But never a gentleman.

Since she'd reentered his life she'd become his dream woman. He wasn't going to tell her, but other women paled when compared to her. Which was why he'd decided to marry her.

The music had switched off sometime when Rae-Anne left. And it didn't seem very festive in CJ's apartment anymore. But it did feel wintry and cold. And he wondered how he was going to make things right. His father's words rang in his ears. *It's our job to protect the women.*

Tad knew he'd done a poor job of that today. He lit a fire in the fireplace and put on a Bing Crosby Christmas CD.

He didn't like to hear CJ talk about herself like she wasn't good enough for any man. He only hoped his long-ago comments weren't to blame. What the hell had happened to her while they'd been apart?

He wasn't leaving until he had an answer. He pushed his way into the kitchen stopping when he saw CJ leaning against the counter with her arms wrapped around her waist and her head tucked down. His arms ached.

"Are you still here?"

"Yeah, and I'm not leaving until we get some things straight."

"What things?"

"One—I'm not like every other guy you've ever met. Two—you don't have any idea what my dream woman looks like. And three—you promised dinner."

"Not now. Okay?" she asked. The vulnerability in her eyes made him want to find the bastard who had hurt her and tear him apart. He stopped thinking about questions and answers and instead went to her and took her in his arms.

He held her tight, savoring the feel of her against his chest. She kept her own arms wrapped tight around herself.

"We are going to talk."

She drew an unsteady breath and he knew she wasn't going to acquiesce to his wishes easily. Too damn bad. Somehow he was responsible for making the spitfire he'd met in the office into this quivering mass of femininity. He had no idea how to change her back. But he was going to try.

This was precisely why he'd decided on an unemotional entanglement with the opposite sex. A marriage of his convenience and her pleasure. It was simple really.

"Cathy Jane, what's wrong?"

"Nothing."

"Women always like to talk about how men don't communicate but y'all could give lessons."

"You sound like your dad."

"Hell, I feel like my dad must when my mom is giving him the cold shoulder."

"I'm not giving you the cold shoulder. I'm just asking you to leave me alone."

"Same difference," he said. His dad wasn't one to talk about emotions but last spring when his mom had had a breast cancer scare, his dad had told him that he couldn't live without his wife. Tad didn't want to believe that he couldn't live without CJ but he knew that Cathy Jane had touched something deep inside him years ago. Something he hoped was mutual that bound them both together.

"We're not married," she said quietly.

The crackle of the fire and the lighted Christmas tree made him wish things weren't complicated with CJ. Made him wish he could take that afghan off the back of her couch, the one he knew her Aunt Bessie had made, and lay it on the ground. Then he'd lower her down on it and make love to her until the shadows in her eyes had disappeared. "I'd like us to be."

"You are making me crazy. Please don't mention marriage again."

"Give me a good reason not to," he said.

"We don't know each other."

He leaned closer to her and brushed a soft kiss against her lips. "Then let's get to know each other."

He scooped CJ up in his arms and walked back into the living room. He sat in the armchair nearest the Christmas tree and put her in his lap with her legs over one of the arms and her head resting against the back corner.

"This is more like it," he said.

"What is?" she asked, her eyes were glassy and he knew whatever she was battling was overwhelming.

He dipped his head and brushed a soft kiss against her forehead. She made him want to cherish her. He didn't understand it. He'd come into the condo with a plan—convince CJ to marry him, maybe cement that decision in bed. But this tenderness, this damned protectiveness she called from him, he didn't understand.

"You...offered up like a feast."

She gave him a half grin then hauled back and punched him in the arm. "Will you stop it?"

This was his old Cathy Jane. This woman he could handle. But that didn't change the fact that something had happened earlier to hurt her and he didn't have a clue what it was. "What happened before? I've never seen a woman react the way you did to a simple marriage proposal and a kiss."

"Nothing with you is simple, Tad."

"You're making this more complicated than you

need to. What happened to the girl I knew in Auburn-dale?''

''She grew up.''

''Growing up doesn't necessarily mean barriers.''

''Well it does for me.''

''Talk to me, CJ. Tell me what that means.''

''I just forgot something that I shouldn't have.''

''What?''

She bit her lip and looked away. He wished she trusted him enough to tell him her secrets.

''You don't have to tell me now.''

''Tad, this isn't going to work. I'll call Butch and tell him to assign someone else to your account.''

''Don't be ridiculous. I told you I'm going to marry you and I'm still determined to make that happen.''

''I'm not marrying a man who isn't my image of the perfect man.''

''Tell me what the qualities are.''

''It's not a list of things you can go out and buy.''

''What is it then?''

''Just a feeling I'll get deep inside when I know it's right.''

''Love?''

''Maybe. It's kind of this indefinable thing that I'll know when it happens.''

She stood up and crossed to the front door. She opened it and Tad got to his feet reluctantly. ''You owe me a dinner. I'll be back at six to pick you up.''

''Do we really have to do this?''

"Hell, yes. Love is overrated and I'm going to prove it to you."

He bent down, took her mouth swiftly and deeply and walked away.

# Five

Christmas had never really been CJ's favorite time of year. Mainly because her mom used to try to make them into the perfect little family during the holiday season. And that had just made her dad's absence more obvious. She knew her mom had everyone's best interests at heart. CJ wondered some times if that wasn't why she tried so hard to make everyone believe she was an image of perfection instead of a real human with faults and weaknesses.

Tad had sent a car and a dozen long-stemmed white roses for her at 6:00 p.m. Standing on the street with a light snow falling, cold wind seeping into her clothing, and a bouquet of sweet-smelling flowers in her arms, she debated getting into the limo.

Tad scared her. More than she'd thought an old high school friend ever could. It wasn't like she really had that many friends from the good old days, she thought wryly.

"You okay, ma'am?" the driver asked.

She hated being called ma'am. For God's sake she wasn't even thirty yet. Way too young to be called ma'am. Except today she felt old and wary. *Very wary.* Hell, too wary for a woman her age. She should be able to enjoy an attraction with the opposite sex instead of being afraid of it.

But fear was part of the allure for her. Her body was pulsing in time with the music in her head. Slow, steady sex music that she'd ignored for a long, long time. Only tonight she didn't want to ignore it and that's precisely why she wasn't getting in the car.

"No," she said to the young driver. "I'm not okay."

She pivoted and walked back in her building past the doorman with the curious expression. The ride up in the elevator was painfully slow, but the car finally arrived at her floor. The condo she called home had never looked more like the sanctuary it essentially was.

She put her key in the lock and made up her mind. She wasn't going to get back on the merry-go-round that had lead to her near destruction with Marcus.

If standing Tad up cost her a promotion at work, so be it. Her sanity meant more than her job. At least right now it did. And she'd started over before. It was actually something she felt she'd mastered.

Her apartment was warm and welcoming after the cold street. She changed into jeans and a thermal shirt and then lit a fire in the fireplace. Glancing in the gilt-framed mirror over the mantel, she scarcely recognized herself. She'd changed a lot in the process of trying to find herself. She'd thought she knew who she was but a wind from the past had shattered her sense of self. Now she saw a woman who vaguely resembled the image in her head and that hurt.

She put on a Christmas CD and puttered around her apartment turning on the tree lights and trying to shake off her mood with seasonal cheer. Not even a cup of apple-cinnamon herbal tea helped. Without thinking, she climbed up on the counter and opened the cabinet above the fridge.

There sat an untouched box of HoHos. Why she liked them she didn't know. They had no nutritional value. They didn't even taste good if you savored them. She pulled the box down along with the un-opened bottle of Bailey's.

Taking the snacks, the liquor and a snifter, she made her way to the living room. Thank God her mother hadn't lived to see her daughter alone and afraid at the age of twenty-eight, reduced to spending her evenings with a bottle of after-dinner liqueur and children's snack cakes.

The music inside her head changed to a frenzied Mozart concerto with layer after layer piled on top of each other. In her mind she knew the layers were job, past, Tad, family and somewhere buried deep beneath the frenetically playing music was Catherine Jane, the real Catherine Jane. Not Cathy Jane or CJ. Just a girl who didn't really know who she was or what she wanted.

After forty-five minutes of analysis she realized she was waiting for something. Waiting for…someone.

She reached for the HoHos box but dropped her hand. She wasn't going to eat her way back to a size 16 over some guy. Except that Tad wasn't just a guy. If he was she'd have gotten into the limo and gone to dinner with him. There was no pressure in dating a man she wasn't attracted to. It was only the men who touched a deep emotional chord inside her that made her quiver with awareness.

She went into the kitchen and started baking. The doorbell rang two hours later when she was in the middle of her grandmother's famous pineapple cheesecake. She hesitated.

Checking the gingerbread cookies baking in the oven, she walked slowly toward the door.

She'd bet money that Tad was on the other side. She'd been waiting for him to come but when she opened the door she found instead a take-out deliveryman.

"I didn't order anything," she said.

"It's a gift."

He opened the heat-sealed container and handed her

a bag of food and a note. She tipped the deliveryman and he left quickly.

She took the bags into the kitchen and opened them. Inside was a meal of Peking chicken and fried rice. The note had been written by Tad.

*Enjoy dinner on me, since you wouldn't have dinner with me.*

She shivered a little. Felt like a big coward and knew that she'd hurt Tad. Something she'd never really intended to do. But she'd had no choice. She couldn't risk losing herself again to the one man she'd never been able to forget.

Tad pushed himself hard in the weight room in his condo. It took the edge off his anger. Anger he didn't have another outlet to release.

If he'd been at his folks' place in Florida he would have visited one of his high school buddies and started a fight with him. There was nothing like a good fistfight to get rid of rage. But they were miles away.

He'd known that he was moving too fast for CJ. But standing him up—hell, that ticked him off.

Women confounded him. He'd never really understood what Kylie had wanted from him until she'd walked away. He didn't really understand why his mom was obsessed with grandkids. And most of all he didn't understand why Cathy Jane Terrence—who dressed in suits, looked like she'd stepped from the pages of *Style* magazine and called herself CJ—was afraid to have dinner with him.

The phone rang but he ignored it. Leaving the weight room and going to the kitchen, he filled a glass with filtered water and drained the cup. In the other room he heard his machine pick up. Heard his own voice telling the caller to leave a message and then CJ's voice. Soft and tentative.

He wasn't going to listen to her message. Hell, when she was finished he was walking into the office and deleting it without listening to it. Tad Randolph wasn't a guy she could manipulate whenever she felt like it.

But he found himself walking down the hall in time to hear her say she was sorry. *She was sorry. Damn.* It sounded like she was on the verge of tears and without really thinking about it, he grabbed the handset.

"CJ?" he asked.

She took a deep breath and then in a husky voice said, "Oh, you're home."

He didn't know what to say to this woman who he wanted to marry but wouldn't let himself love. The woman who had more walls than he knew how to scale. The woman who had become the one he wanted. "I was working out."

"Um…I just wanted to thank you for dinner. That was really nice of you," she said.

Tad knew he could hold onto his anger and let this relationship go no further or he could let it go and try to understand why Cathy Jane always ran. "No problem."

Silence buzzed on the open line. Why had she called tonight?

"Listen, we need to talk," she said, as he heard pans clatter in the sink. Then water running.

"I'll say."

"Are you going to listen or be mad at me?" she asked. The water shut off. He pictured her in her kitchen. In his mind she wore those tight jeans she'd had on earlier.

"CJ, I sat at a table for two in a very expensive restaurant waiting for you for over an hour."

She took a deep breath. "I'm sorry."

"Yeah, right. Why'd you agree to have dinner with me?" he asked. But his mind wasn't on his anger. Lust had kindled to life the minute he'd realized she was in the kitchen where he'd kissed her. He could still feel the softness of her curves against his body. His blood ran heavier.

"You were pushing too hard."

Not as hard as he'd wanted to or else they'd both be in his bed right now instead of in their own houses having a tense conversation on the phone. "I was, but you know I wouldn't force you into anything you didn't want to do."

"I guess."

"Are you afraid of me?" he asked. He didn't think she was. The way she'd kissed him this afternoon told him that she didn't fear him on an instinctual level.

"I don't know."

"I'm not the same guy you used to know." Whatever happened now, he refused to leave things in the weird limbo they'd been in since the last time they'd seen each other in Florida. He liked the woman CJ had become. Liked that she was a successful businesswoman. Liked that she was sassy and smart and sexy as hell.

"Well I'm not the same girl either."

He leaned against his desk. What was she driving at? She'd hinted earlier that she'd changed. But then when he'd given her the opportunity to tell him or show him, she'd chickened out. "I know. What can I do to convince you I'm not a monster?"

"I don't think you're a monster."

"Then what's going on here?" he asked.

"I've never been able to deal with desire well," she said in a shaky voice.

"I don't understand."

"I want you."

His groin hardened and his entire body started to pulse in time with his heartbeat. He straightened and paced around the room. "I want you too. So what's the problem?"

"You want to marry me," she said.

"I'm not following," he said. She made him feel like an idiot sometimes.

"I've never been able to handle a committed relationship and have a life at the same time."

"I'm not planning on taking over your life."

"No you wouldn't plan on it. But it would happen all the same."

"Why do you think that? I don't want to run your life," he said. He meant it, too. He'd learned a long time ago that women need their space. He just wanted someone to share the success he'd achieved.

"What do you want from me?"

"The future. Our future. Not one where we live separate lives but one where we're together."

"That sounds so easy."

"It is. Trust me."

*Trust him.* There was a part of her that wanted to just give in and do whatever Tad asked of her. She'd always liked strong-willed men because life around them was blissfully effortless.

That was why she didn't trust herself. Not Tad. Tad was still the great guy she remembered. But he made her forget who she'd become.

"It's not that simple." She paced the length of her kitchen searching for an escape to the memories Tad's deep voice evoked.

"Sure, it is," he said. His confidence nearly undid her resolve. He'd been right about other things before. Things like which schools to apply to. Which classes to take at the community college over summer.

"Tad…"

"You're weakening. I know you are," he said.

She smiled to herself. The kitchen counter was covered in freshly baked goods and she reached for the royal icing to assemble the gingerbread house from the pieces she'd made earlier.

Her mother, Marnie and she had made two hundred gingerbread houses one year to raise money for presents. God, she'd hated the smell of gingerbread that year. But now it made her feel nostalgic and warm inside. She'd made the house so many times over the years that the work was mindless and she assembled the house feeling her mom's spirit with her as she worked. "What do you want from me?"

"You keep asking me that. I want marriage." He'd been angry when they'd first gotten on the phone. She'd heard it in his voice. But now he was teasing her. He was more relaxed. She was glad. She regretted leaving him alone in a restaurant.

She didn't want to be responsible for him feeling that way ever again. "I'm not going to change my mind."

"Leave that to me."

"Are you sure you want to try?" she asked. Marcus had left her shattered and she wasn't sure she wanted to risk herself again. She didn't want to be back in that emotionally desolate place again.

She'd had to leave her job and start over with another company at the bottom. She didn't want to do it again. And on the emotional side she cared for Tad in a way that she never had with Marcus. Marriage had sounded like a business transaction when Marcus had mentioned it but it sounded so right when Tad did. Maybe that was why she was fighting so hard to keep him at arm's length.

"Hell, yes. The best things in life are the ones you have to work for. Haven't you found that?"

She pushed a row of M&M's into the roof of her gingerbread house. Her career was the only thing she had in her life. She had nice possessions and a house that was the only place where she let her guard down. It had taken her three years of saving and living in a shared three-flat in a so-so neighborhood before she'd been able to move here. "I can be really stubborn."

"I've seen that side of you. And I think I can get around it."

"How?" she asked, absently licking the icing off her finger.

"With a kiss. Babe, you were putty in my arms."

She set down the icing bag and stood up. If he hadn't kissed her today. If she hadn't kissed him then it would be so much easier to walk away. But the powerful desire arching between them was the one thing that had been missing in her life. And she needed him. It scared her. The emotional connection or the physical bond, one or the other, would be okay but not both. "Yeah, I was."

How had he guessed? But then she thought that maybe when you stood a guy up and then confessed to wanting him that he might suspect that you had dating issues. Heck, she had more than issues, she had phobias and she wasn't sure she wanted to explore them with Tad. He made everything about her life seem sharper. She hated lying so she changed the subject. "Will you be in your office tomorrow?"

"I'm not going to stop asking," he warned.

Stubbornly, she refused to say anything else. Finally Tad sighed. "Yes, I'll be in my office. Why?"

"I'm going to send some cookies over."

"Homemade ones?"

"Yes. I've been baking all night."

"Did you figure anything out while you were riding the range?" he asked.

She laughed. That was definitely a Mr. Randolph comment. Tad's dad used to tease her about all the time she spent in the kitchen cooking for Tad when they'd been friends. She'd always liked his folks. They had the kind of marriage that made young girls dream some day they might find their true love and live with him.

"The only conclusion I came to was that I didn't want to hurt you again."

"You can't," he said.

She felt small when he said it. And didn't really know how to respond to him. "Oh."

"I didn't mean it in a bad way."

"There really isn't a good way to take that."

"You're not the only one who's been hurt," he said, softly.

She hadn't thought of that. She'd been so focused on protecting herself she hadn't thought that Tad probably was doing the same thing. Perhaps that was why he'd proposed the marriage of convenience with her.

"Are you sure you want to pursue this?" she asked.

"This? What are you talking about?"

"A relationship," she said, knowing he was being deliberately obtuse.

"I intend to pursue you, Cathy Jane. The rest will work itself out."

He hung up and she leaned back against the counter feeling the first tinge of hope that maybe this relationship would be different from the rest.

# Six

"**H**old the elevator," CJ called as she entered her office building. Plagued by fevered dreams of her and Tad making love in her kitchen with gingerbread houses all around them, CJ woke late and had to rush to make it to work on time.

She'd called her office but Rae-Anne hadn't taken the phones off voicemail. She was more than a little concerned that things were going to be a mess in her office on this Monday morning.

A large masculine hand blocked the doors and she entered the car, juggling purse, briefcase and scarf. She glanced up to say thanks and met Tad's bright green eyes.

"Good morning, CJ."

"It hasn't been good yet," she said. Seeing him now seemed an extension of the dreams she'd had last night. The spicy clean smell of his soap surrounded her. He wore an Icelandic sweater that brought out his eyes and made him look like a Norse god. And she wanted nothing more than to move closer and confirm that he felt as good as she remembered. But she was at work and Tad didn't belong here.

"Let me see what I can do about changing that," he said as the elevator doors closed. He tugged her into his arms and tilted her head back.

His warm breath brushed against her cold cheeks and she knew this was something that had been missing from her life for a long time. She refused to think about it, having decided on her cab ride to work that she was going to take whatever Tad offered her physically.

Slowly he lowered his head, taking her mouth with his in a deep drugging kiss that soothed the frantic pace of the morning. She responded eagerly in his embrace, holding him closer to her. Sensation spread throughout her body. He backed her up against the wall of the elevator car, his big body surrounding hers.

She felt small and very womanly in his arms. He groaned deep in his throat and thrust deep in her mouth, tasting her with languid parries of his tongue.

He slid one leg between her thighs and she rocked her hips against his jeans clad thigh. One of his hands traveled down her back and squeezed her hip, urging her to keep moving against him.

Her breasts felt full and heavy and she shivered, needing more. She pushed her hands under his sweater and felt the warmth of his back through the layer of his cotton T-shirt. She scraped her nails down his back and he groaned again. He was hot and hard between her legs. And she wished she'd worn a skirt to work today instead of pants.

The elevator binged. Tad cursed under his breath and moved away from her. Dazed, CJ had no idea where they were for a minute. But it came rushing swiftly back to her. "My God, I'm at work."

Tad picked her purse and briefcase up off the floor and handed them to her. His lips were swollen and his eyes narrowed on her body. The flush of arousal was on his face and she knew he was as flustered as she was.

"You make me forget everything I've learned in the last five years," she said.

"Like what?" he asked. There was an intensity in his gaze that made her shiver.

"That men and work don't mix."

"Same tune different verse, Cathy Jane. You've been saying that to me every time I get too close and I'm still not buying it."

"Do you want an account manager who is so easily distracted?" she said.

"You're right," he said.

His words cut her but then she didn't really expect anything less. "I'll ask Butch to assign someone else."

"I don't want anyone but you. You're very good at what you do," Tad said with a wicked gleam in his eyes.

He gestured for her to exit the elevator and she did, grateful to see that the hall was empty. She hurried to her office but then slowed as she realized it might seem to Tad that she was running from him. And she'd decided to take control of the attraction between them.

She stopped in the kitchen area and selected a decaf cappuccino from the coffee machine. "So, what are you doing here?"

"I'm here for you," he said in his husky morning voice. She crossed her arms over her chest and scooted away from him. He was too tempting. She wanted to say yes to the vague innuendo in his voice and drag him down the hall to her office, close the door and finish what they'd started in the elevator.

The crotch of her panties was damp, her heart was pounding, her nipples tight and only time or a quickie was going to give her a reprieve. And she didn't want anything quick with Tad. She wanted long hours spent together on a comfortable mattress.

"Don't look at me like that or I'm going to kidnap you and say to hell with the contract negotiations."

"Contract negotiations?"

"That's why I'm here."

Dammit. She closed her eyes and tried to will her mind back to business.

"Here's your coffee," Tad said, handing her the foam cup.

Tad pushed a button to select his drink and she suddenly realized she didn't care how cowardly it looked she had to get away from him. She wasn't in any position to talk to him about terms this morning. She edged toward the exit.

"Where are you going?"

"I need some time to get myself together for this meeting."

"You aren't prepared?" he asked.

Great, on top of everything else, now he thought she was incompetent. "I am. It's just you've rattled me."

"Only fair since you do the same to me."

"Tad, we have to work together. Let's put that first, okay?"

"We are but I thought we decided last night to test the waters."

"What did you have in mind?"

"Pierce and I are having our annual rock climbing race at the store this afternoon. Why don't you stop by for that and then we'll go grab some dinner?"

She watched him, afraid to be alone with him, but needing to more than she'd expected. "I'll be there. But this morning let's just concentrate on work."

"For now," he said and started down the hall to the conference room. She watched him walk away and felt the pressure of his presence tightening in her gut. She needed to figure out what she wanted and take control of this thing with Tad before it destroyed her.

* * *

The meeting with CJ's group went well and afterward she'd rushed back to her office without saying a word. Satisfied with the agreement he'd gotten from her in the coffee room earlier, he'd let her escape and returned to his office in the flagship P.T. Xtreme Sports store on Michigan Avenue near Water Tower Place. His office was on the third floor of the building they leased and overlooked the busy retail floor.

They had a rock-climbing wall that was busy with kids and other tourists taking a break from shopping to work out something other than their wallets. He and Pierce were scheduled for their annual rock climbing/light decorating competition.

Despite the fact that Pierce was a paraplegic and had lost the use of his legs during a fall on Mt. Hood, he still climbed. Pierce refused to let his disability change his life. Tad credited Pierce's outlook and drive as the influence that had made him stop feeling sorry for himself and take charge of his life.

Pierce used his massively strong arms and upper body to pull himself up the rock wall. It was incredibly hard to do—most climbers used their legs for balance and strength but Pierce had refused to give up the lifestyle he loved and had learned to climb without the use of his legs.

It was time for the event to start and Tad had a feeling he would be stood up again. This time he wasn't going to be gentlemanly about it. He was going to CJ's house as soon as the event was over and he wouldn't leave until she told him why she kept running away from him.

The local media were here to cover the event and he and Pierce had both been interviewed earlier. They also had a tree-lighting ceremony that featured the state champion long distance runner from a local high school. The entire affair was innocent but then again so was riding in the elevator most of the time.

"Ready, old man?" Pierce asked from the doorway.

Tad was beginning to think it was past time to throw in the towel where CJ was concerned. "Yeah, I guess so."

"What are you waiting for?" Pierce asked.

He grabbed his harness and climbing shoes and walked out of his office. "Not what. Who."

"Am I supposed to understand that?" Pierce kept pace in the wheelchair, pushing it with his muscled arms. The chair rolled past Tad and into the waiting elevator.

"Nah."

"How'd the meeting go with the new advertising company?" Pierce asked. Pierce was in charge of product development and would be working closely with CJ and her team. He had just returned from a two week vacation in Montana where his family owned a large cattle ranch.

"Good."

"I'm still not sure we made the right decision."

"You've seen the presentation boards. I know they'll do a good job."

"If you say so."

"I do. You know I'm always right when it comes to these decisions."

"I know you think you are. Remember last year you said the Bears would go all the way."

"I remember you saying the same thing about the Falcons."

"Better not let this get out or we'll look like we don't know a thing about sports."

"I was right about opening this store."

"So you had one good idea," Pierce said.

His cell phone rang before he could respond. "Randolph."

"It's CJ. I'm on my way to your store but traffic is heavy."

"I wasn't sure you were coming."

"I said I would."

"You've changed your mind before."

"Not anymore."

"Promise?" he asked.

"Promise," she said, disconnecting the phone.

Pierce watched Tad with a shrewd gaze. Tad didn't want to talk about CJ with his friend. Pierce had said on more than one occasion that Tad had horrible taste in women. He didn't want Pierce's opinion on CJ.

"Who was that?"

That was the thing about working with your best friend. Pierce felt free to poke his nose into all of Tad's business. "No one."

"The woman you were waiting for, right?" Pierce

asked. He maneuvered the wheelchair around as they approached the ground floor.

"Pierce, I don't meddle in your personal life."

"Enough said. Ready to get your butt kicked by a handicapped man?"

Pierce had won the past three years. And it wasn't because Tad let him win. Pierce was a fierce competitor who'd honed his body into a winning machine. He spent a good portion of the year winning wheelchair road races. "You bet."

They entered the crowded showroom. "I'll take the media while you set up the gear and lights."

"Gotcha."

"Need some help, *compare?*"

Tad glanced over his shoulder surprised to see Rae-Anne at the shop.

"What are you doing here?"

"Working, believe it or not. I'm supposed to get a feel for your company's work ethic. All of CJ's team is here tonight."

He was surprised to hear it but shouldn't have been. For CJ the job always came first. He had a feeling that if they had dinner tonight it wouldn't be just the two of them. "CJ's a hard boss."

"You have no idea the half of it. Women are...demanding."

Tad laughed. "You should know."

Rae-Anne muttered something under her breath and reached for a string of lights testing them. "What's the point in doing the event?"

"One hundred percent of tonight's profits go to area schools' nonvarsity sports programs. We get a lot of traffic and this gives the customers' kids something to do while they shop."

"I'm impressed."

"Let's hope CJ is too," Tad said.

"Still waiting for hell to freeze?" Rae-Anne asked.

"Yes."

"Anything I can do?" Rae-Anne asked.

"Mind your own business," CJ said, coming up behind them.

CJ knew that old chestnut about listening at eaves but she'd never been able to help herself. Rae-Anne shrugged and walked away. "Talking about me?"

Tad pivoted to face her. His eyes lingering on her lips. She knew he wanted to reach over and kiss her but wouldn't with all the people around them. She was tempted to lean over and kiss him instead. Anything to shake him up in this environment where he was way too confident.

He shrugged and gave her a half smile that went straight to her heart. "Just soliciting help from your faithful secretary."

"You need help?" she teased, moving closer to him. He'd changed and was wearing shorts and a T-shirt. He looked like the buff sports guy he was and she wanted him.

He leaned down, his cologne surrounded her and

when he spoke his warm breath brushed her cheek. ''Not really but I figured any extra couldn't hurt.''

Awareness spread throughout her body pooling in her center. She wished she could go back in time to this morning in the elevator. She'd hit the stop button and make love to him. Then there wouldn't be this anticipation running through her veins and filling her with excitement. Then she'd be able to concentrate on her job. On learning everything she could about P.T. Xtreme Sports instead of focusing on the sexy co-owner.

But that wasn't going to happen, so she patted his butt and scooted away from him. ''I don't think you're going to need anything extra.''

He threw his head back and laughed drawing many, appreciative feminine stares.

''You like what I've got?'' he asked, closing the gap she'd opened between them.

''What do you think?'' She'd forgotten what it was like to play this teasing game. To let anticipation build until it was a fevered pitch and neither of them could wait a moment longer.

''Cathy Jane, you always keep me guessing.''

That made her feel in control and more sure of herself than she should around Tad. ''Good. You're too cocky for your own good.''

''Too cocky?'' he asked, arching one eyebrow at her.

She titled her head to the side and gave him the once-over. His athletic shorts revealed his muscled runner's legs. She skimmed her gaze over him starting at his well-worn climbing shoes and not stopping until she reached his head. "Yeah, you know that attitude that says I'm a buff-macho-man-in-control-of-his-environment."

He canted his hips to one side. "I'm giving all that off?"

Now she felt a little silly. "Well, not all that but you know what I mean."

He cupped her face and kissed her quickly but fiercely. She shivered as he pulled away. "I know you make me so hot I can't think of anything else but you."

"Really?" she asked.

"Really."

"Good. It'll keep you on your toes."

He chuckled again, turning to adjust his harness and then step into it. "Better watch that sassy mouth. It's going to get you in trouble."

The vee of the straps on his thighs drew attention to his groin. She could tell she'd had an effect on him. With a wink, she said, "That kind of trouble I can handle."

"Is there any that you can't?" he asked, moving closer to her.

Teasing and lightness were the key to managing Tad. She wasn't sure, but she thought he might be content with the facade she showed the world instead of trying to see the real woman she hid. "None that you have to worry about."

"Who says I'd worry?" he asked, buckling the harness and then wrapping the lights he and Rae-Anne had straightened earlier into a neat coil. He put the lights into a pouch and fastened it to his belt.

He looked every inch the primal man she knew him to be. Tad was the kind of frontier man who would have been able to support his family with no one else around. He was a survivor and that appealed to her because if the past ten years had taught her anything it was that she was a survivor, too.

"I knew all that testosterone had killed the gray matter."

"Cathy Jane, you are playing with fire," he said, leaning close to her once again. She grabbed his harness and pulled him closer. His pupils dilated and she knew she was playing a dangerous game.

Though the store was crowded they were isolated together. They stood on the other side of the barrier that separated the public from the climbing wall.

"What are you doing?" he asked, his voice low and husky.

"Checking to make sure your harness is tight."

"Why?" he asked.

She'd needed to touch him again before he climbed the wall. It was kind of high and she didn't want Tad falling. "Because you've got all the trouble you need right here with me."

"Now that you're here, I can handle anything you throw at me. It's when you're running that you give me difficulty."

"Are you sure you know how to do this rock climbing thing?"

"Oh, I know exactly what I'm doing on the wall."

"What is the point of this?" she asked.

"Climbing to the top stringing the lights and then rappelling back down. All before Pierce of course."

"Pierce is your partner?"

"Yes."

"Is he any good at this?" she asked. What kind of competition was this going to be? From the job perspective this could be just the thing they needed to give Xtreme Sports the edge.

"He's second best," Tad said.

"You wish," a man said.

CJ turned to see a very well-built man in a wheelchair. He had kind eyes and was wearing a harness like Tad's.

"Cat Girl meet Pierce. Pierce, this is Cathy Jane Terrence."

"Cat Girl?" Pierce asked, glancing up at her.

She knew she was going to regret that name from the moment she'd met up with Tad. But as she stared at him, very much at home in his environment she realized she didn't regret having him in her life again.

# Seven

"That name is a long story and one that needs to stay in the past. Please call me CJ," she said, taking the hand Pierce held out to her.

Pierce took her hand and brought it to his lips, kissing her hand. "It's a pleasure to meet you. I like stories, tell me about this name of yours."

CJ flushed and Tad realized that their inside jokes were meant to stay inside. And he knew that the name, which had been her rebellion against a group of peers who didn't see beyond her outer shell, was still a point of vulnerability with her. Why hadn't he realized it before now?

"We knew each other in high school. That was her nickname then," Tad said at last.

CJ gave him a surprisingly grateful look. Did she still not trust him?

"I can see where you got that nickname. You are sexy, but I am surprised high school boys would have been able to appreciate the nuances of your charm."

CJ shrugged and Tad remembered how he hadn't made her life any easier during that time. Her expression made Tad want to carry her away from Pierce and the crowded store. He wanted to find a secluded place to apologize once again for the idiot he'd been as a boy. To promise he'd make up for all the hurt she'd endured as a teenager.

"What was your nickname?" Pierce asked.

"None of your damn business," Tad said. Rad Tad had ruled the school and he'd been very aware of his position in the small pond that Auburndale Senior High was. He'd loved being the guy everyone knew or wanted to know.

Pierce watched CJ with more than just passing interest. Noticing Pierce's reaction to CJ, Tad realized he wasn't going to be content to let things develop slowly in the way that CJ wanted. He needed to brand her with his name.

He wanted every man who looked at her to realize they were poaching on his territory. And he knew that screamed of machismo and that CJ would never let him live it down if he gave her any indication of how he felt.

She was his—dammit. On a very elemental level he and CJ had bonded and he wasn't going to let her go.

Tad reached down and tugged her hand free of Pierce's. CJ lifted both eyebrows at him in question but he ignored her.

His past relationships had shown him one thing. He liked the challenge of going after a woman just out of reach. Was that the appeal with CJ? His gut said there was much more involved than that.

Frustrated, he glared at Pierce. As soon as he did, he saw the amusement on his friend's face. All this talk of high school had obviously made him revert to that eighteen-year-old behavior. All the experiences he'd gained with women fell away and he felt exposed and raw in front of CJ.

Being ribbed by Pierce for his behavior was insignificant compared to the jealousy running through him. Branding CJ was the least of the things he wanted to do to her.

Usually Tad was amused by Pierce's old-world manners. In fact, Pierce had flirted all the time with Caroline his last girlfriend and that had only amused Tad.

"CJ Terrence from the ad agency?" Pierce asked.

"The very same," CJ said.

Tad wrapped his arm around her waist and pulled her firmly against him. Her soft curves cushioned against his body, distracting him from the conversation. Too much time had passed since he'd held her in his arms.

"I didn't realize you two were personally involved," Pierce said.

"Actually, Cathy Jane's the woman I'm going to—"

"Say it and I'm going to plant a kiss on Pierce's lips he'll never forget," CJ warned.

"Say it," Pierce urged.

"Forget it, buddy." Tad tugged her back and dropped a quick kiss on her full mouth. He tipped her chin up and stared into her eyes. "Not saying it doesn't change my plans."

"What plans?" Pierce asked. His friend was enjoying this a little too well for Tad's liking.

"Nothing. Let's get this rock climbing thing done. CJ and I are going to dinner."

"Sounds good to me," Pierce said. "I'll go make the announcement."

Pierce rolled away and Tad checked his gear one more time. He hoped the climb would distract him from the new feelings spreading through him. Marrying CJ was one thing, caring for her something else, something he wasn't sure he could control and he didn't like that.

The strong emotions she inspired were intolerable. This was a woman who'd been running from him since the moment that they'd met again a few weeks ago. And Kylie had proven to him that chasing after a woman did nothing but make him look like a fool.

Tad had to be able to let her go. He refused to end up like Pierce had when Karen left him. Sitting alone in a dark room with only a picture album and a bottle of Cutty Sark. Using cheap booze to push away memories that he thought would last a lifetime.

*Keep it light.* He could do that. Hell, he had a history of keeping things light.

"Give me a kiss for luck?" Tad asked CJ.

She hesitated. "I kind of invited my staff to go to dinner with us."

Tad knew that despite what she'd said to him earlier, she was still running from him. Running from something he made her feel?

"I'll get Pierce to join us as well. What were you planning to discuss?"

"At the time I was afraid to be alone with you. But now…"

"Now?" he asked.

"I think I might have sabotaged myself. Because I can't wait to be alone with you."

"Promise?"

She leaned up and hugged him tightly to her. He forced himself to let her control the embrace but he wanted—hell, he needed—to crush her to him. To keep her close to him so that she didn't change her mind.

"Promise," she said in his ear.

Dinner at the Cheesecake Factory had been a noisy affair. CJ's staff had a million ideas and Pierce had been a jovial host spurring them on. Halfway through dinner Pierce's significant other, Tawny O'Neil had joined them. The leggy blonde had dropped onto Pierce's lap and planted one hot kiss on his lips.

Tawny had been funny and watching her and Pierce together had made CJ long for something she'd never had. A real relationship. One that was based on mutual desire, respect and affection.

Tad by comparison seemed quiet and brooding. And now that they were sitting in his car outside her condo building, she wasn't sure how to proceed. So much had changed between them and yet her fears remained.

"Alone at last," Tad said.

She wanted to smile at him and keep it light. He was just a guy. Just an ordinary guy. But he wasn't. And she'd always known that.

Sleeping with Tad was the biggest risk she could take. Because she was already half in love with him. He embodied so many of the qualities she wanted in her Mr. Right. Cementing their relationship by making it a sexual one was all she'd thought of since this morning when he'd kissed her in the elevator. But he wanted something from her she'd promised herself she'd give no man.

"Second thoughts?" he asked, tracing one finger down the side of her face.

"Not really. It's just that now that we're alone, I'm not sure what to do."

His features were illuminated by the dashboard lights and in his eyes she searched for some emotion that he felt but couldn't acknowledge. She saw tenderness and desire. Was that enough?

She was trying so hard not to let her body control her life again. And she realized that protecting herself from being hurt might be a bigger risk. Was it a risk she was willing to take?

He leaned close to her; his breath brushed her cheek. Her face still tingled from the rough rasp of his fingertip. Awareness spread throughout her body, pooling in her center. She shifted on the seat, clenching her thighs together.

"Invite me up for a cup of coffee," he said. He had no doubts. Maybe she was thinking about this too much.

She tilted her head to the side. Inside her the heavy beating of lust awoke. Each beat of her heart seemed louder and fiercer than the one before it. Her clothes felt constricting.

Tad's breathing was shallow as well. His nostrils flared and pupils dilated. Her mind noted every masculine detail and she realized that there was no turning back. She'd made up her mind earlier in the day.

"Want some coffee?"

"Hell, I want more than that," he said.

"How about something sweet with your coffee? I still have some cookies, pies and cakes I baked the other night. Is that enough to satisfy you?"

"You're all the dessert I need."

She hesitated with her hand on the door. "Am I really?"

Tad framed her face with both of his hands and

brushed his lips against hers. "Are you having doubts again?"

"You already asked me that."

"I want you to be very sure of this, Cathy Jane, because once we make love everything will change."

She swallowed. She knew that it would. And perhaps that was why she was hesitating. But she couldn't live the rest of her life in fear of a man's touch. Afraid that she'd indulge the passionate side of her nature at the cost of her sanity.

"No doubts."

She got out of the car and led the way into her building. The doorman smiled and waved at them as they waited for the elevator. She hadn't brought any man up to her place the entire time she lived here. Finally the doors opened and they entered the car. Tad pressed the button for her floor and as the doors swooshed close, pulled her into his arms.

He smelled good and it felt right to be in his arms. Every sense was attuned to him. His scent embedded deep in her hungry soul. He rubbed his hands down her back, cupping her buttocks and bringing her body more fully against his.

He possessed her with a complete attention to detail that left her burning for more. She turned her face toward his, seeking his mouth but he evaded her. Stroking his lips over her face.

His mouth settled on her neck. Teasing her with soft biting touches that made her forget everything but him. Her world narrowed to just the two of them.

When the doors opened on her floor it seemed natural that he'd lift her in his arms and carry her down the hall.

He set her on her feet in front of her door. He watched her with narrowed eyes. He was aroused and wanted her with an intensity that warned her her time for running was over. Her body said good, she was through with running. But her heart warned her to be careful. That the price to be paid for passion was a high one.

''Open the door, CJ,'' he said. His voice was deep and raspy and she knew he was on the razor's edge as well. That for him reason and caution were being superceded by instincts older than time.

Knowing she wasn't alone in these tumultuous emotions reassured her. She took her key from her purse and unlocked the door.

Glancing over at him, she wondered what he would do when he realized that she wasn't the innocent girl he remembered. When he realized her fears stemmed from perhaps too much knowledge of herself and not an uncertainty of what sex with him would be like.

''Last chance to run,'' he said.

She wasn't running from Tad anymore. Or from herself. The past few years had been cold and lonely and she wasn't going back to them again.

Taking his hand in both of hers, she opened the door and pulled him inside. She pushed the door closed and backed him up against it. She brought his mouth down to hers and laid both of their fears to rest.

* * *

CJ took his mouth in a kiss that was deep and carnal. She tasted him with languid strokes of her tongue, exploring him as if she meant to leave no secrets between them. As if she meant to uncover all of his desires. But he wasn't eager to play the passive role.

He returned the thrusts of her tongue with his own. Tilting his head to the side for better access, he cupped the back of her neck, supporting her while he savored her mouth. She moaned deep in her throat and shifted restlessly against him.

His erection lengthened and he nudged his hips forward, thrusting one leg between her thighs and nestling his too purple flesh against her. Frustrated by the barrier of clothes between them, he pushed her coat and his to the floor.

Reaching between their bodies, he unfastened her blouse. Her bra was lacy to the touch and her nipples hard little stones. He tore his mouth from hers and stared down at her in the dim light. She was exquisite. Her body pale alabaster.

Her fingers worked busily at his shirt as well. Raking her fingernails down his chest, she gave him a smile as old as time. He let her explore his chest for a few moments, savoring the arousal spreading throughout his body. She leaned down to nip at the skin that covered his pectoral with her teeth and then went lower to suckle both of his nipples.

Her mouth on his nipples sent a pulse of pure fire through his groin. His erection tightened, becoming painfully full. This wasn't going to be a soft gentle seduction. He needed more. And he needed it now.

Using his hand under her chin, he tipped her face up to his and kissed her again. And then she was rocking against him, her breath coming in short gasps. He pulled away.

With one hand he unfastened the front clasp of her bra, but didn't push the cups away from her skin. He felt her breath catch in the back of her throat. Knew she was anticipating his next touch.

He wanted to bend down and take her hard nipples in his mouth. But he waited until he was sure she was aching as much as he was for the touch. He circled the areola carefully, watching her squirm as he did so.

"Like that?" he whispered against her neck, right below her ear.

"Oh, yes," she gasped.

He slid his mouth down the column of her neck stopping at the base to suckle against the wild pulse beating there.

She grasped the back of his head and held him to her. Her lower body gyrating against his. "Tad…"

He bent and moved lower. Nibbling along her skin until he encountered the cups of her bra. He traced the edge where fabric met flesh with his tongue. Goose pimples spread across her chest. And her grip on his head tightened.

He cupped her breast in his hand. Molding and lifting the globe, he turned his head and blew lightly on the tip. She shivered again.

He hovered over her aroused nipple letting his hot breath bathe her flesh. When he touched her with the tip of his tongue, she moaned his name again.

She was on the brink of orgasm and he wanted to see her go over for him. Wanted to see the moment when pleasure infused her entire being. He unfastened her pants and pushed them down her legs.

CJ unfastened his pants and pushed her hand inside, stroking her hand down his length finally cupping his balls. She squeezed gently and he almost came. But he wanted their first orgasm together to be hers. He lifted her in his arms and carried her to the couch.

He set her down on the soft cushions. She leaned forward and he could feel her breath on his groin. He groaned. He wanted her mouth on him. "Not yet."

Gently he pushed her panties down her legs and then arranged her so that she was spread out on the couch for his consumption. He slid one of the pillows under her hips so that she lay before him like a scrumptious feast.

"This is what I call dessert," he said, reaching between her legs, he fondled her humid flesh with long slow strokes.

Carefully he pushed one finger into her channel and she moaned, her fingernails digging into his shoulders. He slipped a second finger inside to join the first.

She was so wet and ready for him. But he didn't want this to end too quickly. He dropped openmouthed kisses on her stomach and abdomen. Then trailed his mouth lower. Her hands were in his hair once again.

He glanced up at her. Some women didn't like a man's mouth on them in such an intimate way.

''Okay?'' he asked.

She bit her lip and nodded.

She smelled musky and womanly and he couldn't wait another minute to taste her. He parted her with his thumbs. Her pleasure center was thick and swollen and he teased her with his breath and lips. He continued working his fingers inside her body.

With his other hand, he plucked at her nipples and stroked her from neck to waist and back again. Her hands moved restlessly up and down his back and as her tension grew her touch became more frantic. He stopped caressing her body and held her hips with both hands. Tasting her deeply until he felt her clench around his tongue.

She cried his name out loud and her body shook in his hands as she came.

He lifted his mouth from her and stood. Then lifted her and carried her down the hall to her bedroom. He placed her on the center of her bed and removed his clothes before climbing in next to her and pulling her into his arms.

He pushed her open blouse and bra from her body and savored the feel of her in his arms. His stroking hands rekindled her desire. But when he tried to roll her under him, she pushed against his shoulders and he let her force him onto his back.

She straddled his hips and rose over him. His sex was still rock hard and he could feel her wetness against him. Thrusting upward he teased himself with her warmth. He moaned out loud. He needed to be buried hilt-deep inside this woman. Now.

''Not so fast, Rad Tad. It's time for my dessert.''

# Eight

"Dessert, am I?" he asked with a mock frown.

Leaning over him, CJ licked her lips. "You are more tempting than anything in my kitchen."

She had Tad in the one place she'd always wanted him—her bed. Even though he'd brought her to climax on the couch, there was still an unnamed emptiness inside her that only complete possession would satisfy.

She wanted him to fill her. She wanted to engage his senses the way he had hers, sending him beyond anything he'd felt with any other woman so that he'd always remember her. She wanted to brand his soul the way he was marking hers.

But she wanted to do it on her terms so that she could protect the woman deep inside her. The woman who'd always been susceptible to her appetites and who'd never really learned to say goodbye to her dreams. The woman who was very afraid that Tad was going to realize one day that CJ was no more than a facade.

She wouldn't allow herself to be that vulnerable. She caged his wrists in her hands, holding them on the pillow next to his head. Tad said nothing only watched her through narrowed eyes. His penis stirred against her moist center, letting her know he enjoyed the change in roles.

She lowered her body until they were pressed together, propping herself on her elbows she stared down at him. His eyes were languid as if he had all the time in the world and there was no urgency. But his heart told a different story, beating frantically beneath her chest.

She leaned down and kissed him. Taking her time and finishing what she'd started at the front door. He tried to take control of the embrace, lifting his hands. But she forced them back to the bed.

CJ nipped at his bottom lip in warning. He returned to his supine position but she knew that it wasn't her will dominating him but his desire to let her dominate him.

She hadn't meant to tease him when he'd given her such pleasure earlier. "What do you like?"

"With you, everything."

She smiled. That was one of the nicest compliments she'd ever received. "Good. Lace your fingers together and keep your hands under you head," she ordered.

He did as she commanded. She rocked back on her heels, still straddling his body. He was a strong man with an athletic build. "Wait here."

"I'm not going anywhere," he said.

She hurried into the bathroom and grabbed her massage oil and a box of condoms from the medicine cabinet. She also picked up a box of matches and lit the candles on her dresser when she reentered the room.

Tad had propped three of the pillows on the bed under his shoulders and now reclined on the bed like a pasha awaiting his harem girl. It didn't matter that she'd told him to wait there for her, his presence dominated the room.

She placed the box of condoms on the nightstand before sitting on the bed near his hips. She lifted the small brown bottle that contained a sandalwood scented liquid.

"What have you got there?"

"Just some oil. Do you mind?"

"Not at all."

She poured a small amount into her palm and rubbed her hands together. Then leaned over him. Rubbing the soothing lotion into his skin. His muscles under her hands were hard and strong. But he was putty in her hands.

She massaged her way down his torso, taking the time to explore his bare upper body. The hair on his chest tapered down to his groin. She poured a small puddle of oil low on his abdomen and then rubbed it downward. His body twitched as she moved lower. She teased him by massaging his thighs and then working her way further down his left leg.

She massaged his feet and then moved back up the right side of his body. His hips moved restlessly as she neared his groin again. This time she shook two small drops onto the swollen flesh. His breath rasped between his teeth as she worked her hands over him rubbing until all the oil had been absorbed into his skin.

Straddling him again, she bent over him until she could caress him with each undulating twist of her body. His penis was hot and hard between her legs. Each circular motion of her hips brought him closer to her entrance. She felt him tense underneath her each time she brought him closer and closer to her center.

"I need more," he said.

"How much more?" she teased, rubbing the tips of her full breasts against his chest. He moaned and rocked his hips up towards her, seeking entry.

She stretched over him to reach the box of condoms. While she fumbled to get one from the box, he latched onto her nipple and suckled her. She dropped two condoms before she finally had one. She reached between their bodies and put the condom on him. Then stroked his length a few times until he sat up and grabbed her hips.

Holding her still, he thrust upward and into her. She gasped at the size of him, he was bigger than she'd expected. Her sheath stretched to accept him but she felt too tight.

''Come on, baby, you can take me,'' he said. He rubbed her back in large circles and soon her body had adjusted to the too-tight feeling of having him inside her.

''I can't wait any longer,'' he growled against her neck.

He thrust upward into her, pulling her hips down to meet his. His pace increased until they were both frantically striving toward the pinnacle. Her nipples abraded his chest with each thrust. He suckled at the base of her neck, whispering hot sex words against her skin and urging her on. Telling her she was beautiful and sexy. The most woman he'd ever held in his arms.

She held his shoulders and caressed his back. He slid his hands from her hips to her mound, touching her exactly where she needed to be touched. And sending her over the edge. She cried out his name as he gripped her hips harder and thrust up into her once, twice and then came with a shuddering growl that rocked her bed, body and her world.

She lowered her head and rubbed her cheek against him. His heart thudded under her ear and she closed her eyes for a moment savoring his closeness and memorizing his scent.

The scent of sandalwood still lingered in the air when Tad opened his eyes the next morning. CJ was full of surprises and secrets. He hadn't expected the sensual massage she'd given him or her aggressive behavior in bed. Taking a strand of her hair in his hand, he brought it to his nose and inhaled deeply. Arousal spread slowly through him. They'd made love twice more in the night and though he should be satiated he wasn't. If he had his way he'd keep her in bed for at least a month.

His stomach growled. He knew it was close to dawn because of the sunlight creeping in under the closed window blinds. He scanned her room for a clock but couldn't find one.

Her bedroom was an oasis of calm prints and Asian inspired furniture. The candles she'd lit last night were thick chunky ones in muted tones. And the large mirror over her dresser showed the two of them on the bed. He leaned up on his elbow to see them better.

The expression on his face was fierce. He looked like a predator. By contrast CJ looked like prey laying underneath. Cursing under his breath, he rolled to his back.

He stretched his arms over his head. The more he came to know CJ the less he really understood her. She was complex and deep, revealing the important details of herself grudgingly.

But last night had opened his eyes. He'd come to realize that CJ used more than dyed hair and contacts to keep the world at bay. She'd also hidden the sensual side of her nature.

A woman who hid from the world. A woman who was trying to protect herself.

Had he played a part in that? Had his careless comments more than ten years ago wounded her in some way that she'd never recovered from?

He glanced over at her, she faced away from him. Her long hair curling on the soft cream-colored pillowcase. The feminine curve of her back called to him. He reached out and traced a pattern over her skin.

She was so soft and so fragile, he thought. Sleeping next to him her guard was down and her vulnerability was apparent. Rolling onto his side, he pulled her toward him, wrapping his body completely around her.

He wanted to wake her up and vow to be her protector. To make a noble speech the way knights of a more chivalrous age had. But he wasn't a chivalrous knight. He was a twenty-first century man who had vulnerabilities he didn't want the world to see.

Marrying her seemed more dangerous now than it had before. The first time he'd proposed it had been straightforward. He liked her, he wanted to sleep with her, she was someone his parents would adore. But these new protective urges she was inspiring puzzled him.

She moaned a little in her sleep, shifting in his arms. Her buttocks rubbing against his hardening shaft. He swept his hands over her body, and she mumbled in her sleep again, undulating against him.

''Wake up, sleeping beauty,'' he said, nuzzling the vulnerable curve of her neck.

''Tad?'' she asked.

''Who else would it be?''

"No one else," she said. She rolled over to face him. Her hands came up to cup his jaw. Her fingers stroking over his beard stubbled cheeks.

She was pliable right now, still more asleep than awake. Leaning down he kissed her. She twisted against him, bringing her thigh up over his hip. He thrust against her center. Not entering her just letting them both feel each other.

He rocked them both back and forth, bodies moving together until they climaxed. It wasn't a huge world-rocking orgasm like the one they'd shared in the night, this one was more suited to the soft morning. He tucked her closer to him.

"This can't be real," she said.

"It can be."

She groaned, opening her eyes. "Please don't bring up marriage now."

"Why not?"

She tried to push away from him but he refused to let her budge. "Tad."

"I'm not letting go until you talk to me. I know there's more to your hesitation than the flimsy reasons you've given me."

"How do you know that?"

He shrugged. He wasn't sure of the right words to use. The ones that came to mind felt crass and too harsh for the woman in his arms.

"Why is this so important to you?" she asked turning the tables.

He didn't want to talk about himself. But she stared

at him with those deep brown eyes of hers. "Uh…it's complicated."

"My point exactly."

"I'm not like you—afraid of marriage. It's just that…I'm going to sound like a sap when I say this."

"I won't think you're a sap," she said, leaning up to kiss him.

At least she wasn't trying to leave the bed. He took a deep breath. "Have you been home lately?"

"Not in four years. Marnie lives in St. Louis and my mom's buried in Orlando so there's no reason to go to Auburndale. Why?"

"My mom's been having some heart problems, she spent three weeks in the hospital last summer."

"I'm sorry to hear that. What does she have to do with your wanting to marry me?"

"My parents are tired of waiting for grandkids and are always bugging me to settle down. Until my mom went into the hospital I didn't take it seriously. I felt like I had all the time in the world, but I don't. My folks are older and this would make them happy."

She leaned up on her elbow. "What about your happiness?"

He grabbed her and pulled her down on his chest. "I'm happy with you."

"Really?"

"Really. You're so open, honest and fun-loving."

"You sound like a personals ad."

A niggling thought at the back of his head warned him that things weren't going as smoothly as he thought they would. He knew he should tell her more—maybe let her glimpse that dream he had in his head of her as his wife and two little kids playing at their feet. But instead of being quiet he said, "You're just what I want in a wife."

She pushed out of his arms and stood next to the bed. "But I'm not any of those things."

She pivoted and walked out of the bedroom into the connecting bathroom, slamming the door behind her.

CJ stared at herself in the bathroom mirror. She scarcely recognized the naked person reflected there. It had been a long time since she had love bites on her neck and beard burn on her breasts.

Her thighs were pleasantly sore and her center was still a little dewy from her latest orgasm with Tad. He was a generous and skillful lover.

She'd known that if she slept with Tad everything would change between them. She'd been prepared to let him see a part of herself she normally hid from the world. What she hadn't been prepared for though was realizing that she'd shared her body with a man that didn't even realize she hid anything.

She fingered the mark on the bottom of her neck, remembering how he'd suckled her there before he climaxed that first time. What was she going to do? If they were having an affair it wouldn't matter. But he wanted marriage—to make his ailing mother happy.

She raked her hands through her hair. What was she going to do? Bracing her hands on the counter she leaned in close to the mirror. But no answers came to her. Frustrated by her thoughts, she stepped into the shower.

She let the hot water steam the room before she opened the glass door and got inside. The water washed over her, sluicing away the doubts and the fears racing around in her mind.

One fact kept resurfacing, Tad was the kind of man she'd been secretly searching for. Which made him doubly dangerous to her. She liked that he worked hard to make his life a success. She liked that he was community focused. She liked that family was important to him. The only missing ingredient was that Tad saw her as the kind of woman she could never be.

That he thought she was open and fun-loving made her wonder if she really gave off that impression. Didn't he realize she'd never let anyone see the real her? That her work persona was one huge superficial layer that she used to make everyone believe she belonged there. In the office she was successful and energetic because that's what she needed to be to achieve her career goals. It was a role she played, an outer shell to protect the woman she was inside.

They'd had deeply soul-satisfying sex, she thought. She'd realized last night when she'd held him under her that there was more to Tad than any other man she'd taken to her bed. More than Marcus who'd taught her what pleasure could really be. She'd seen the man Tad really was and recognized layers still existed between them.

Frustrated with the world in general she wanted to scream but didn't. She took her loofah and angrily soaped it up. Scrubbing Tad from her body with rough strokes of the sponge. Except that even after she'd cleaned her entire body, she could still smell him on her. The shower door opened and a blast of cool air entered the stall with her.

Tad stood there naked and unsure. The way he watched her told her that he knew something was wrong between them. Understood that she wanted something more from him—but had no idea what it was.

She didn't know if she could do this. Maybe there was a reason why secret crushes usually weren't realized. Perhaps some people weren't meant to be more than a far-off fantasy. Her heart ached a little at the thought that this was probably the end for them.

"Ah, baby. Don't look at me like that," he said. He rubbed his hand on his chest through the patch of hair there. He smelled of sandalwood and sex. Primal instincts urged her to say to hell with forming a relationship, just grab him and make love to him again.

But her heart was weary. "Like what?"

Tilting his head to the side, he watched her carefully for a moment then said, "Like I've disappointed you."

She crossed her arms over her chest to protect herself. "Well you have."

"How?"

She'd forgotten how hard it was to talk to men. "If I have to tell you it won't mean anything."

He threw his head back, cursing savagely under his breath. Finally he looked at her again. "I can't read your mind."

She knew what he meant. But she didn't like letting anyone know she had any insecurity. It wasn't just Tad, it was any person. Even her sister Marnie who'd seen her at her lowest now believed that CJ was a fabulously successful ad executive. "I'm not expecting you to."

"Then tell me what the hell I did wrong?"

She just shook her head. How could she tell him that he didn't know her? That she wasn't the woman he remembered or the one he thought he knew. That she was an amalgam of them both and a silent third woman that lived deep inside her soul.

He sighed, stepping into the shower and closing the door behind him. He took the loofah from her hand and dropped it to the floor, then pulled her into his arms.

He tipped her head back and lowered his mouth to hers. The kiss he gave her was filled with masculine impatience and a tenderness she didn't know he was capable of.

After a few minutes, he lifted his head. "What's wrong?"

His gray-green eyes were so serious and patient. She had the feeling he'd hold her like this for an eternity until he received the answers he was seeking. Dropping her head, she mumbled softly, ''You don't know me at all.''

''You haven't let me.''

# Nine

**A**fter CJ got out of the shower. Tad grabbed her soap and washed himself. He wasn't going to keep chasing her. He'd done that with other women before and had been left with empty arms. CJ had changed a few images in his head last night. Marriage, though still important to him, might not be the right thing with her.

He turned off the water and dried off. He used CJ's razor to shave and nicked himself twice. Hell, this wasn't his morning. He wrapped the towel around his waist and entered her bedroom.

CJ stood in front of her mirror wearing a silk bathrobe. He watched her tame her wild curly hair into a neat looking ponytail. Then she applied her makeup and put in her contacts. She passed over the jeans and sweatshirts in the closet and chose instead a pair of camel colored wool trousers, an ivory cowl necked sweater and some fancy ankle boots.

Watching her dress was like watching a transformation. And he realized what she'd meant earlier. He hadn't realized how much of herself she hid from the world. But that didn't mean he didn't know the real woman.

She took a strand of pearls from a teak jewelry box and put them on. Then added matching earrings. Still he could only stare at her.

She was donning her armor, putting layers of clothing between them. He was tempted to say the hell with it but his gut said getting her out of his system wasn't going to be as easy as walking out the door.

"It's not going to work," he said at last.

She glanced over her shoulder at him. Lipstick pencil in one hand, eyebrow raised. A haughtier look he'd never seen on her face. It made him want to throw her on the bed and slowly peel each of those flimsy layers away until all that was left was the naked writhing woman who'd left his arms.

"You can't ignore me until I go away."

"Why not?" she asked. She'd turned back to the mirror and painted her bottom lip with a deep red hue. Only the fine trembling of her hand showed him there was a chink in her protective covering.

"Because we have unfinished business, Catherine Jane Terrence. It started that first day you moved in next door and fell off your bike. Remember that?"

''Yes,'' she said.

''I gave you my Band-Aid and told you I'd always be there for you.''

She looked away from him. ''But you weren't.''

He crossed the room to her, put his hands on her shoulders and met her gaze in the mirror. She put the lipstick pencil down.

''I am now. Or at least I'm trying now. You have to meet me halfway.''

''I know. You're right. I haven't let you close to me.''

''Why not?''

She fiddled with the makeup brushes on her vanity. ''I don't know.''

He turned her to face him. She looked too sleek, too sophisticated for the woman he'd come to know. And yet he realized this side of her personality was as true as the stirring lover he'd held in his arms last night. ''Don't know or don't want to tell?''

She squared her shoulders. ''Don't want to tell.''

''You can trust me.'' He opened his arms, inviting her into his embrace.

She turned away and paced a few feet from him. ''No. I can't.''

Tad couldn't play this game anymore. He wanted her. He was willing to try to work through the problems between them but he was a man. He needed to know what was wrong so he could fix it. And this guessing game wasn't doing anything but frustrating him. "This is getting us nowhere. I thought you said you'd meet me halfway."

"I'm trying."

"And I'm leaving. When you're ready to be reasonable, call me."

He donned his clothes quickly and CJ stood quietly, watching him.

He walked out of her bedroom and was aware of her following him down the hall. Her pants and shoes were on the tiled floor of the foyer. Her panties lay next to the couch. He remembered the shattering intimacy he'd felt when they'd mated and he didn't want to leave.

He wanted to take whatever she'd give him. But he wasn't some wimpy guy who'd hang around until she was ready to give him whatever crumbs of affection she was willing to throw his way. He couldn't deny her allure. He knew if he had the opportunity he'd sleep with her again. He also knew that wasn't the solution.

"Tad, don't go."

Instead of looking at her, he stared out the window. A light snow fell and the sky was cloudy and gray. Perfect weather for snuggling by a fireplace except the woman he'd chosen to get involved with wasn't interested in cuddling. "Give me something that will make me stay."

"I'm afraid," she said. Her words were faint, he went to her but didn't touch her. He knew himself. She'd said the words that conjured up all his latent protective instincts. The ones that made him want to slay dragons for her.

"Afraid of me?"

She shook her head. "Never of you."

"Who then?"

She twisted her fingers together and bit her lower lip. "Myself I think."

She stood in her living room. The Christmas tree behind her, homey pictures on the walls and instead of looking at ease in her sanctuary she looked frightened.

"I don't understand."

"You know how I said you don't know the real me? I don't either. I've been reinventing myself for so long that I'm not sure who I am."

"And that scares you."

"Partly. The other part that scares me is that you make me want to forget all about who I've always wanted to be and make myself into what you want in a woman."

"My wants are simple, Cathy Jane."

"They are?"

"Yes, I want you to marry me."

She shook her head. "No man has ever stayed."

He was humbled by her words. This woman was eons too soft for the world she lived in. This woman was waiting to see what he'd say, expecting him to brush her concerns aside and walk out the door. This woman he realized had been hurt in the past and badly.

Don't let me screw this up and wound her, just when she's coming to mean so much to me.

"Which men?" Tad asked.

CJ was sorry she'd opened her mouth. She wished she could go back in time and wake up again. She'd make love to Tad and then when he was in a weakened state, then she'd get out of bed and make him breakfast. Plying him with lots of food and sex until he was unable to think or ask her questions she didn't want to answer.

He held her with patience and she had the feeling he'd stand there all day until he got the answers he craved.

"Why don't we sit down?" she asked.

"Okay."

CJ awkwardly moved out of his embrace. He was so strong and comforting, she was tempted to stay there in his arms, hiding from herself and the past. But she couldn't. She had made a history of running when things went to hell, and she knew this time would be no different.

He was being too solicitous. It made her feel unreasonable and silly. She knew that wasn't his intent but it didn't change the way she felt. Glancing around the room, which still bore signs of last night's seduction, she shivered a little. They couldn't talk with her clothes everywhere.

Why couldn't there be some sort of magic that made embarrassing details like her panties disappear?

"Let me clean this up," she said.

"I'll help," he said.

"No."

CJ picked her clothes up off the living room and foyer floors. His stomach had growled twice.

"Want to go grab some breakfast?"

"I can cook something for us. We can talk while we work." She wasn't ready to face anyone else. And she was ready to trust Tad. To tell him a little of her past relationships with men, starting with her dad who'd left them long before the Terrence women had moved to Auburndale. Left them for a teenaged Lolita and made it very clear that the last thing he'd wanted to be saddled with was a wife and two daughters.

Marcus had left her for another woman as well, but he'd done it in a much quieter way, suggesting she leave the ad agency where they'd both worked to avoid embarrassment. Now Tad was tempting her to risk a little of her heart and see if he'd reciprocate.

"Let's eat first."

In the kitchen she boiled water and put the grounds into her French press. The silence was deafening, probably because she knew that she needed to talk to him about her past. About Marcus and her dad and how she'd never really trusted any man when he said he'd stay. And they never had, proving her right.

She flipped through the CD wallet on the counter and selected one by Ella Fitzgerald. Soon the sultry jazzy sounds filled the air. She turned nervously to find Tad staring at her.

"I guess you want to talk."

His stomach growled.

"Or not. Hungry?"

"Yeah. I wake up that way. Where do you keep your frying pan?"

She pointed to the cabinet. "What are you going to do with it?"

"Make breakfast," he said. He retrieved the pan and then opened her fridge.

"You can cook?"

"Don't sound so incredulous. I'm a bachelor. I don't like eating takeout for every meal."

"Sorry. What are you going to make?" she asked. He seemed so offended she wondered if he'd had some chef training.

"Fried eggs and bacon. You can handle the toast."

She rolled her eyes. She couldn't believe she'd let him make her feel guilty when all he could cook was a camping breakfast. "I don't know that you can call that cooking."

"Don't get sassy, Cathy Jane, or I won't let you have any."

"My heart might thank you."

He threw his head back and laughed. CJ smiled to herself as she squeezed oranges for juice and made toast. The lingering tension in her stomach disappeared as they worked.

Tad served them eggs and they sat at the counter in her tiny kitchen eating quietly when Ella sang about love and heartache. Thoroughly mirroring the sentiment in CJ's heart. She wondered if she should have left the CD player off. This wasn't really helping.

"Not bad," she said. The eggs were perfect and the bacon nice and crisp.

"For a guy, right?"

"Well…"

"That's what I thought."

"You can't take a compliment."

"Were you giving me one?"

"Yes. I was."

They finished their breakfast in silence. Then CJ cleared the table and stared at Tad where he sat watching her. She knew he was ready to talk. That she'd delayed things as long as she could. She poured them both one more cup of coffee and led the way out into the living room.

Settling down in front of the fireplace, she waited for Tad. He sank down next to her on the loveseat. His hipbone, rubbing against hers.

He settled his arm behind her on the back of the couch and then turned toward her. "Where were we?"

"I'm not sure. You wanted to hear about my past."

"I'm not asking you to tell me any big secrets, CJ."

"I know. But I've kind of built it into a big confession."

"It doesn't have to be. I'm sorry that you think I don't know you at all. I am trying but you don't make it easy."

"It's hard for me to let anyone close to me."

"Why is that?"

She shrugged. "I guess it's all tied up with my self-image. I've never really been the right size or look."

"I can understand you feeling that way in high school but you shouldn't now."

"Sometimes I still do."

"Is that what this is all about—looks? I'm not that shallow."

"I know. It's just when you say things like you want to marry me. You bring all those doubts back. Because I know that I can't be the perfect woman for you."

"Why not?"

"There's something inside me that makes men leave."

"I'm not leaving," he said. "I'm planning to marry you."

"So you keep saying," she said.

"I think you made a good point about us not knowing each other."

"I did."

"Let's just date for a while, sound good."

"Sleepover dates?" she asked.

"Definitely."

CJ felt the first ray of hope that she and Tad were really going to have a relationship. He was willing to stay with her. He wanted to get to know the real her. He made her realize that life outside of the advertising world could be good, too.

They spent the afternoon on Michigan Avenue, browsing through shops. He wanted to go into Tiffany's but CJ refused teasingly. And he'd relented about going into the store. But deep inside he wondered if they were both playing a game of pretend.

After purchasing a vase from Crate and Barrel, they strolled toward State Street. Carson's and Field's had their Christmas window displays up. They dined in the Walnut Room in Marshall Fields. A light snow began to fall as they walked back to CJ's place.

The day would have been relaxing for Tad except that he couldn't get the image of CJ as she'd been this morning out of his head. This woman had been hurt badly and he knew he owed it to her to make sure he didn't add to the pain she'd experienced.

But at the same time he was worried about protecting himself. CJ had been dancing just out of his reach since he'd found her again. But he was confident that he could get her to agree to marriage.

His parents were coming up the day after Christmas and his plan was to present CJ as his future wife to them. But suddenly ten days didn't seem long enough. He wondered if ten years would be. Though she hadn't said it, CJ needed something from him that he hadn't yet been able to figure out.

"Penny for your thoughts?" she asked. He held her hand loosely in his and as they walked he shortened his pace to hers. She wore a long camel-colored wool coat, a cream-colored muffler and a pair of black leather gloves.

She fit perfectly in the city and watching her now,

he wondered how she'd ever survived those tumultuous adolescent years in Auburndale. She wasn't a small-town girl. And he'd been a small-town boy who'd never really stopped to notice how that small town could make a person feel. "Just thinking about my folks."

"Are they coming up for the holidays?" she asked, tipping her head back to watch the snow. CJ seemed lighter tonight. Easier to know. And he realized that she'd been more than a little bit accurate about the fact that he'd never really tried to get to know her.

"Yes. Mom grew up in New England and loves a white Christmas."

"Me too. I used to wish for snow every Christmas growing up."

"Every Florida kid does," he said, but there was more to her words than just a child's wishful thinking. There was incredible longing right alongside the knowledge that fairy tales didn't come true in CJ's voice.

"What did you wish for?" she asked.

"The typical things, bikes, cars, video games. You?" He was an only child and though his parents had instilled him with a strong work ethic, they'd also spoiled him on holidays.

"I'm not very materialistic," she said in a tone he was coming to realize meant that she was hiding something.

"You aren't going to tell me?" he asked. Stopping, he pulled them out of the flow of the foot traffic. Under a streetlamp, he pulled her into his arms and tilted her face up towards his.

She looked at him, her heart in her eyes, and he wanted to tell her not to trust him that deeply. He didn't feel worthy of that kind of emotion. ''I used to wish that my dad would be there on Christmas morning.''

''He never was,'' Tad said. He'd never met CJ's dad. Her mom, Marnie and she had moved in one summer. They'd pulled up in a battered station wagon towing a U-Haul and the three of them had moved everything in. Mrs. Terrence had never had any boyfriends and had worked all the time.

When he and CJ were twelve they'd been friends. That entire summer it didn't matter that she was a girl and therefore the enemy. Finally he had someone his own age to play with and they'd spent the long days exploring the orange groves and playing pretend games.

''No. He'd left long before and he wasn't ever coming back. But we didn't talk about that.'' She pulled out of his arms and hugged herself.

''Why not?'' he asked. He wanted to pull her back into his arms but he respected that she needed some space.

''Because it was just easier to pretend he was away for business.''

''Easier on who?''

''I don't know,'' she said at last. ''Maybe Mom.'' She shivered a little, tucking her muffler up higher on her neck. "Sorry. Not what you were wanting to hear, was it?"

"I wouldn't have asked if I didn't want to know. Ready to head home?" he asked.

"Yes."

He wanted to spend the night with her, but didn't know how to ask. And he didn't want to make their time together too heavy. She was too emotional now, he wanted to lighten the mood.

"Didn't you say you studied Tae Kwon Do?"

"Yes."

"Wanna spar?"

"I don't trust the gleam in your eyes. What exactly do you have in mind?"

"Just a friendly game of strip fighting."

"Strip fighting? You've got to be kidding."

"No, I'm not. I'll let you use all your gear. You're not afraid are you?"

"Of you. Never. Where are we going to have this match?"

"My place. I converted my spare bedroom into a workout room."

"Okay, are we betting on this match?"

"Oh, yes."

"What's up for grabs?" she asked.

"Loser cooks breakfast."

She watched him carefully. "I'm going to need some sort of handicap. You look a bit stronger than me."

"Just a bit."

"Yeah, just a bit."

"You're all heart, girl."

"Don't you forget it."

They teased and bantered all the way back home but once he had her in his condo the last thing he wanted to do was spar, so he took her to bed and made love to her all night long until they both fell into an exhausted sleep. But he woke deep in the night and held her tightly in his arms. Held her with a desperation that he'd only admit when no one else could see it. Held her like he'd never let her go.

# Ten

**F**ive days later, CJ was on the top of her game. Rae-Anne seemed to finally understand how most of their office equipment worked and hadn't lost any important documents or disconnected any busy clients lately. Butch Baker had called five minutes ago and she was in the elevator on her way up to meet him.

And if the tingling in her gut was any indication she was getting the promotion she'd worked so hard for. She checked her lipstick in the mirrored elevator walls, straightened the lapels on her burgundy suit and tucked up a wisp of hair that had escaped her chignon.

She smiled at her reflection and repeated her mantra. "I'm successful and everyone wants me to succeed."

The elevator doors opened and she pivoted to exit

the car. She entered Butch's office and his secretary Molly told her to go right in. She squared her shoulders and opened the door.

"You wanted to see me?" She hoped she sounded cool and calm but the pounding of her heart echoed in her ears, so she had no idea how she sounded to Butch.

"Yes, CJ. Come in and have a seat."

She sank into one of the leather guest chairs in front of Butch's large mahogany desk. The walls of his office were lined with many of the most popular advertisements of the past ten years. Anyone who entered this office could easily see why Butch was a top executive at Taylor, Banks and Markim.

The credenza showed a different side to Butch though. Pictures of his wife and kids were there along with the Little League baseball team he'd coached for the past five years. They'd won their division championship this year.

"I'm not going to keep you in suspense, CJ. I asked you up here to let you know you're our newest director. Congratulations."

CJ smiled calmly and shook Butch's hand. "Thanks for your confidence in me. I'm going to work hard to make sure you don't have any regrets about your decision."

"I have no doubt that you will work hard. That's one of the things I wanted to mention to you."

"Working hard?"

"Yes. You almost didn't get the promotion because you have so few activities outside of the office."

"I think that would be a good thing," she said.

"Statistics show that executives that have a balanced life are actually more productive at work."

"What are you saying, Butch?"

"You've worked hard for this promotion and you deserve it. But now it's time to take care of the other aspects of your life. Take time to date, start a hobby, volunteer in the community. Take some time for yourself."

Her stomach knotted and she started to open her mouth. To tell Butch that she was engaged. Hell, it was what Tad wanted. But she couldn't do it. Her job had always been the most important thing to her. Suddenly it paled in comparison to her relationship with Tad. But being with Tad meant taking risks. Risks that she'd never admit to another soul she felt each time she was with him. Risks that were capable of making everything, even this exciting new promotion, seem dull gray.

"I'm not sure I understand, Butch. You want me to get married?"

"Your personal life is your concern. I just want you to do something outside of work. The board likes all their executives married though we can't make that a qualification for the job."

"I'm dating someone now," she said.

He nodded. "Your promotion is effective today and we'll be moving you to a new office on this floor in

January. You're invited to meet the partners tonight at seven for drinks. Why don't you bring your friend?''

''I will.'' She left his office and made her way back to her own. This wasn't happening. She'd gotten her promotion now and they wanted her to change her focus.

She entered her office and Rae-Anne glanced up from her computer. ''Well, are we celebrating?''

''Yes. You are looking at the new director of domestic affairs.''

''Congratulations.''

''Thanks, Rae-Anne,'' she said, entering her office.

She should get the staff together for an announcement and have a catered lunch to celebrate the promotion. She'd have to start interviewing to fill her position. There were so many things to be done, she should be making a list of work responsibilities but she couldn't.

Her mind wouldn't stop. The pressure she faced doubled with Butch's words about balance and... *marriage*. She'd known since she was a little girl, since she'd watched her mother staring at her father's picture every night before she went to bed, that she'd never marry. She'd taken a chance with Marcus and he had left her even though she'd tried to be what he'd wanted in a wife.

Rae-Anne buzzed in on the intercom. ''Tad's on line one.''

''Thanks, Rae-Anne. Call around and see if we can get someone to cater lunch for the staff today. Then get everyone together for an announcement in the conference room.''

"Will do.''

She pressed the button on the phone. "Tad?''

"Hey, Cathy Jane, are you free for lunch?''

"Uh, actually, no. I got my promotion and I'm bringing in food for the staff.''

"Congratulations, you've worked hard for this promotion.''

"Thanks,'' she said.

"I'll take you to dinner tonight to celebrate.''

"Okay. Are you free for drinks at seven?''

"I can be, why?''

"It's this thing with the board and I don't want to go alone.''

"I'll be there.''

He sounded so confident and sure of himself, but that didn't alleviate the pressure inside her. Trusting Tad was the easiest thing in the world because despite the fact he looked like some buff hunk his heart was deep and true. But CJ was afraid to trust Tad. Afraid to trust herself. She hung up the phone feeling like crying instead of celebrating.

The restaurant Tad had selected for their celebration dinner was Gejas in Lincoln Park. They were known for Old World elegance. Tad had heard of the restaurant but had never eaten there. But tonight the secluded booths seemed perfect for dinner with CJ. Their table was along the wall so they could close the curtain and celebrate in private.

He'd stopped by Tiffany's this afternoon to pick up the ring he wanted to give her when he asked her to marry him. But he sensed CJ wasn't ready to be asked again. And this time he wasn't just asking to make his parents happy. This time he needed her to say yes and he wasn't taking any chances. So he purchased an amber and gold bracelet that reminded him of the amber specks in her dark brown eyes instead. The jewelry box was in his pocket and he wasn't sure when to give it to her.

He ordered a bottle of champagne to celebrate her promotion. CJ had been flushed with success during the cocktail hour with the partners of her firm. Frankly he'd been awed and intimidated by her. He'd suspected she would have turned out smart and successful when he'd known her in high school, but never guessed how far she'd go in the business world.

Butch had been surprised that he was CJ's date but had been happy as well. And several of CJ's co-workers had seemed glad to see them together.

The waiter took their order. Gejas was renowned for their fondues. Tad ordered a three course meal for them. Once the waiter poured their champagne he left.

Tad closed the curtain and pulled CJ into his arms. Damn, she felt too right there. And he'd missed her all day. Seeing her for drinks with her co-workers had intensified his need to hold her. There hadn't been time for anything but a quick embrace before they'd had to mingle. But now they were alone and isolated from prying eyes.

"First a toast," he said. He'd ordered a plate of strawberries to go with the bubbly beverage.

"And second?" she asked.

Next was CJ warm and willing in his arms. He had the evening planned. Delicious, sensuous food, warm, sexy woman. What more could a man ask for?

"Second…you'll have to wait and see."

"What if I don't want to?" she asked, lifting one of the berries. Her pearly white teeth carefully held the fruit before she took a bite of it. She closed her eyes and he imagined the deluge of juice flooding her mouth. Unable to help himself, he leaned forward. He traced his tongue over her lips, tasting both the berry juice and CJ. Her mouth parted on a gasp and he thrust his tongue inside. He pulled her closer to him. His arm supporting her neck as he savored her mouth.

"Is this my punishment?" she asked.

"I haven't decided yet."

"Make your toast so we can get on with your discipline."

Tad lifted his glass and stared at the bubbly beverage. He didn't know if he had the right words to tell her how proud he was to be her man. He wished he had Pierce's gift of always knowing the right thing to say. But he didn't have it and he wouldn't want CJ to think he was someone he wasn't. Yet she made him want to be better than he was and he knew he'd changed since they'd been friends and lovers.

"Congratulations, CJ. I'm so proud of everything you've accomplished with your life."

He lifted his glass toward her. But she was only staring at him, a sheen of tears in her eyes. "Thank you, Tad."

"You're welcome, gorgeous. Now take a sip of your drink. I have more surprises for you."

"What? You know I don't like surprises."

"You'll like this one."

"Promise?"

"Just trust me," he said, wishing she'd trust him on more than this night. Wishing she'd trust him with her future. But knowing he'd settle for her present.

She cupped his jaw, rubbing her fingers over the five o'clock shadow dotting his cheeks. "I'm starting to trust you."

"Drink," he said. Her hands on him started a fire that he wanted to put out in only one way. And Gejas, although the booth set up gave couples some intimacy, wasn't the place for the kind of seduction his pounding body demanded.

She took a sip of her champagne and he did the same. Then he took a bite of one berry and fed her the remaining fruits. Sharing each berry brought a flush of desire to her skin. He was tingling from head to toe. His arousal pressed against the zipper of his trousers and he relished the anticipation. Seduction and anticipation had never felt as good with any other woman.

The waiter brought their first course. And once he

left and they were alone again, Tad said, "Tradition says you have to kiss whomever is seated to your left if anything falls off your fork."

"And you are conveniently seated to my left."

"Funny how that happened."

Their meal progressed with a slow steady stream of kisses and sumptuous food. As the second course was cleared away. Tad removed the box from his pocket and placed it on the table in front of CJ.

She stared at the distinctive Tiffany's box. It was long and narrow, so she had to know it wasn't a ring, but still she hesitated.

"Oh, Tad. You didn't have to get me a gift."

"I know. I want you to do me a favor before you open it up."

"What?" she asked.

"Take out your contacts."

"Why?"

"Because you use them to hide from the world. But you don't need to hide from me."

She took a small contact case from her purse and removed the contacts. He reached up and pulled the pins from her hair, letting the thick mass curl around her shoulders.

"Do I look better now?" she asked.

"Not yet," he said. Leaning over he kissed her hard and long. Pulling back only when he knew her lips would be wet and swollen from his kiss. "Perfect. Open your gift."

Her hands shook as she pulled the box toward her.

She opened it slowly as if afraid a snake might spring out of it. But he recognized this vulnerable side of CJ. And it made him want to scold her for not trusting him.

Finally she pulled the bracelet from the box. Tears sparkled in her eyes again and this time fell. ''I...oh, Tad. Thank you so much.''

''You're very welcome,'' he said, taking her hand and fastening the bracelet on her. He dropped a soft kiss on her wrist. And saw trust in her eyes for the first time, and he knew that it was time to take her home and make love to her. Time to push harder at the barriers around her heart, which he sensed were already starting to crumble.

CJ unlocked the door to her condo and entered, turning on the hallway light. This day had been a roller-coaster ride of excitement, fear and joy and pressure and Tad's presence didn't exactly ease those things in her mind.

Her new bracelet glittered with the reflections of the soft lamp. She still couldn't believe Tad had given her such an expensive gift. Coupled with her boss's words earlier, the bracelet applied pressure to her already troubled mind.

Tad ran his hand down her back. Every nerve in her body had been sensitized by an evening of sumptuous food and lingering touches. Her pulse beat low and heavy. The only thing she wanted to do was stop thinking and make love with Tad.

He closed the door. "Let me take your coat."

She shrugged out of her wool coat and felt his warm breath on the back of her neck. He brushed her hair out of the way and dropped an openmouthed kiss there. He took his time stringing together that nibbling contact until she shivered with sensation rushing down her spine and pooling in her center.

"Are you cold?" he asked.

She couldn't answer. He smiled indulgently down at her, and pulled her into his arms, whispering in her ear the things he'd do to make her warm. His hands roamed up and down her back, lingering to cup her butt and pull her more fully into his embrace.

His mouth on her ear made her breasts feel full and heavy. Her nipples tightened against the satin fabric of her bra. She needed more. Leaning fully into the hard planes of his chest, she stood on tiptoe and pulled his mouth to hers. Their kiss was a series of long drugging touches that only intensified the struggle inside her. How could she live with or without Tad? She was flushed with desire when he moved away.

She stood awkwardly in the foyer while he flicked on the lights of the Christmas tree and lit a fire in the hearth. He'd hung his suit jacket up earlier and now stood facing her, back-lit from the fire. He tugged his tie loose and left the ends dangling down his chest.

"Come over here," he said.

She hesitated. She didn't know what to do. Tad had become more important to her than she'd ever thought he would. And tonight she'd seen the way Butch's eyes had followed them. It would be so easy to appease her boss.

"Cathy Jane, why do I get the feeling you're running again?" he asked, softly.

*Damn.* Why had she complained that he didn't know the real her? She didn't want to talk. So instead she started walking toward him unbuttoning her suit jacket. "Does this look like running?"

She shrugged out of her jacket and came to a stop in front of him wearing only her black satin bra and skirt.

"I stand corrected."

"Indeed you do," she said, trailing her fingers down his torso and rubbing his erection. He drew his breath in sharply but stood still for her caresses.

"One of us is overdressed."

"I'd say we both are."

"Let's do something about it." She unbuttoned his shirt and pushed it off his shoulders. She'd never tire of looking at his thick corded muscles and washboard abs.

Tad unhooked her bra and slowly peeled away the satin. He cupped both of her breasts with his large hands. Rotating his palms against her, he brought her nipples to throbbing attention. She tried to think but could only want.

"Tad…"

"You wanted something?" He bent toward her, tracing the rim of her ear with his tongue before drawing that wet caress down her neck.

He used his fingernail to delicately trace around her nipple until she almost couldn't stand his touch anymore. She was incapable of speaking or thinking. Finally his mouth covered her turgid flesh and she sighed. Holding tightly to his head while he suckled her.

He continued to undress her, pushing her skirt down her hips and she felt his surprise when he encountered the bare flesh of her buttocks. He stepped back and she stood in front of him wearing only a brief thong, thigh-high hose and black pumps. He growled and lifted her in his arms.

Settling her on the sofa, he followed her down. His hands and mouth were everywhere. Leaving no inch of her body untouched, he caressed her curves and whispered endearments against her skin. He pushed his fingers inside her panties and touched her deeply and intimately until she was hanging on the edge of climax.

She pulled his hand away.

"Why?" he asked.

"I want us to come together," she said.

He stood and quickly got rid of his remaining clothing. He pulled a condom from his pocket and handed it to her. "I had other plans for this evening."

"What plans?" she asked.

"Something a bit slower but you turned me inside out with those hose."

She waggled her eyebrows at him. "I wish I'd

known it was this easy to rattle you. I'd have tried it sooner.''

"You don't have to try," he said.

He pulled her thong down her legs and tossed it on top of his clothes. She reached for him caressing his thighs and penis. He moaned and she put her hands on his butt bringing him closer to her. She leaned up and tasted him. He moaned again, his hands burrowing into her hair and holding her close. She took the tip of him into her mouth. He tasted spicy and masculine.

"Enough," he said gruffly pushing her back. He took the condom from her and sheathed himself. Then spread her legs and came down over her. He guided himself to her entrance with his hand and then plunged into her with one deep sure stroke.

Even though they'd made love several times, it still took her body a few moments to adjust to the too tight feeling of being filled with him. As soon as she clenched her lower body muscles, Tad began to move between her legs.

His hands left her hips, gliding up her body to her breasts, where he lingered, then to her shoulders. Finally he cupped her jaw. Their eyes met and in his she saw her past, present and future. A shimmering of sensation started at her center and spread slowly throughout her body. Leaving her quaking in his arms. His climax followed hers and he groaned her name before collapsing in her arms.

She stroked her fingers up and down his back and held him with her arms and legs. They were both sweaty and she knew she should be exhausted, but all she could think of was that she couldn't risk staying with Tad. Couldn't risk losing anymore of herself than she already had to this man who easily dominated her entire world.

# Eleven

Tad sent a car for CJ on Christmas Eve. His parents were arriving the next day and tonight he planned a small intimate dinner for the two of them. He'd gone back to Tiffany's and purchased an engagement ring. There was a bouquet of long-stemmed roses in the back of the limousine. He'd called his mother to find out which kind of candles to burn at dinner—unscented ones. He'd purchased some at Crate and Barrel.

He'd also spent some time in Barnes & Noble purchasing a half-dozen different books of love poems. Though he didn't want to risk his heart and actually say the words—he felt them deeply. CJ had pushed past his resolve too far to keep his emotions uninvolved. He loved her and somehow tonight he planned to find a way to tell her.

The food had been prepared by a friend who was a chef at one of the city's most exclusive restaurants. The limo driver called after he had picked CJ up and was on his way. Tad had every thing precisely how he wanted it when CJ knocked on his door.

He opened the door and took her coat. She wore a black velvet dress that ended at her midthigh. Her long legs were bare and on her feet she wore the sexiest pair of spiky heels he'd ever seen. He put his hand on the small of her back to escort her to the dining room and encountered bare flesh.

He slipped his finger between the warm satin of woman and the cool velvet of her dress. She undulated against his touch and he smiled to himself. They communicated so much better physically than verbally.

He had been so nervous about tonight, but suddenly his nerves had disappeared. A surge of lust pierced through him and he thought to hell with this romantic crap which he wasn't all that good at. Bending he dropped a kiss on her bare back. She shuddered under his mouth and he grinned. She was so easy to turn on.

Sliding his hands around to cup her breasts he continued to nibble his way down her back. He tongued the crevice where pale feminine skin met dark velvet. Taking the tab of the zipper in his teeth, he pulled it lower.

He continued kissing his way down her back, lingering at the small indentation right above her buttocks. Finding her naked under the dress made him moan. She shuddered and he tasted her lower. He wanted to take her like this, from behind up against the wall.

He stood and pressed his straining erection against her. She swiveled her hips against him. He reached between their bodies to free his throbbing length. Rubbing his penis against the curves of her naked buttocks. She moaned. "Tad."

He cupped her breasts through the cloth of her dress. She was caged by him. His mouth on the back of her neck, his hands on her breasts and soon he thought when she was a mass of quivering nerves, he'd penetrate her and make her his completely. Take her so deeply and so thoroughly that when he finally asked her to marry him, she'd have no choice but to say yes.

He pulled her more firmly against his chest. He slid the straps of her dress down her arm just far enough so that the bodice gapped and her pink nipples were framed in velvet. He turned her in his arms, and backed her up against the wall.

Taking her wrists in his hands he pinned them to the wall behind her. And though he knew it was illusion, at this moment she seemed to be totally his. The hard berries of her nipples beckoned him and he bent to tease her first with his warm breath, then with his wet tongue.

She tasted incredibly sweet. The scent of her perfume was stronger in her cleavage. He let go of her wrists for a moment to plump her breasts together and bury his face between them.

He turned his head from side to side trailing wet kiss over the full globes. She trembled in his arms, her hands falling to his shoulders, her nails biting into his flesh. She was close to the flash point. It was only fair since he felt in that state constantly around her.

She moaned his name and shifted her thighs, pressing them together. He thrust one of his legs between hers. Grasping her wrist with one of his hands, he used his other to urge her hips forward.

He pushed her skirt to her waist and thrust his hips forward until he settled her feminine notch over his penis. He resented every time he'd worn a condom because he'd never been able to savor her humid warmth against his skin. He hardened painfully and could count his pulse in his erect penis.

He switched his attention to her other nipple, pulling at it in search of some sustenance that he only found with CJ. He'd never tell her but when she was in his arms, she soothed a deep troubled part of his soul.

He stroked between her thighs, not entering her body, just teasing them both with the promise of what was to come. He lifted her completely off the ground.

''Put your legs around my waist.''

''Yes.''

Wrapped in her strong slender thighs, nails raking down his back and her mouth under his. He shifted his position and entered her.

A sigh of satisfaction escaped him. This was where she belonged—writhing in his arms. The urge to mate with her and claim her was so strong that he ceased thinking and just indulged his senses.

He thrust hard and deep into her. She nipped at his lower lip, pulling it between her teeth and suckling it. She ripped at the buttons of his shirt and she scraped her nail over his nipples. The added sensation made the base of his spine tingle. He felt so full, so hard and so heavy. He was going to come any moment. But not without CJ. He reached between their bodies and stroked her until he felt her body clench around him. He thrust into her once more and then joined her climax. His body emptying in jetting pulses.

He twisted so his back was against the wall and sank to the floor cradling her in his arms until their pulses slowed. CJ slid off his lap to sit next to him on the floor. They both leaned against the wall head turned to face each other. Her hair was in disarray around her face and he looked into her deep brown eyes.

"I'm sitting on something."

"What?" he asked.

"This," she said, pulling the Tiffany's box that had been in his pants pocket out.

She stiffened but didn't say a word.

"I was going to surprise you with that after dinner."

She continued to watch him with eyes that were too wide and too serious.

"Will you marry me, Cathy Jane?"

* * *

CJ's heart beat so loudly she thought she might pass out. There was too much pressure involved with her saying yes to Tad. At once it was a dream come true and a nightmare. Not just because of the way she felt about Tad but because of the way she knew she was when it came to men.

"I'm not letting you off the hook again. I know you, dammit. I know that you put your hair up and put in contacts when you go to work so that everyone sees a smart, sophisticated woman. I know you wear jeans and T-shirts at home because they are comfortable and suit your quiet lifestyle. I know you bake when you're upset and that you'd rather read books than go to a bar."

He pulled her back into his arms and she couldn't help herself. She snuggled against his broad chest. "I know you, baby."

She knew him, too. Knew that Tad needed more from her than she could give. More than she'd ever really be willing to give because the risk to her heart was too high. Though she wanted his love, craved his body and lived for the times they were together, she couldn't marry him.

And she knew this time she'd have to tell him more than she was afraid.

"I can't."

"Is it because of your job? I respect what you've achieved. Hell, you know I'm proud of you."

"No, it's not that. In fact, Butch urged me to find

a spouse and marry. He's concerned I don't have enough balance in my life.''

''He's right. You don't.''

''There's a reason for that. Tad, I don't juggle well.''

He ran his fingers through his hair. ''So if it's not work then what is it? The emotional thing again?''

He grabbed his pants and stood up. Pulling them on he put his hands on his hips and canted them toward her. He was tough and angry-looking, a man anyone would be afraid to face alone but she'd never felt safer.

She straightened her dress and got to her feet. She struggled with the zipper until Tad brushed her hands away and pulled it up. He put his hands on her shoulders and turned her to face him.

What she saw in his eyes made her shiver with longing and an unnamed fear. Actually the fear had a name and she had a healthy respect for it. Because she knew that once she started depending on Tad he'd leave. Fate had made it plain that CJ Terrence wasn't supposed to have a continuous male influence in her life.

''I love you, Cathy Jane. I've never said those words to another woman.'' He watched her steadily. She felt the force of his will surrounding her. She wanted to reach out and take. Reach out and touch him. To go back to a few minutes earlier before she'd sat on that damned ring box, but she couldn't.

''That's not enough for you, is it?''

''Please don't do this. Can't we go on as we have?'' she asked.

"Damn you, CJ, no we can't. You're not the only one who's been hurt. Look at Pierce, his wife almost destroyed him when she left but he's happy now with Tawny."

"I don't care about Tawny and Pierce. I mean I'm glad they're happy but how can you understand what I'm going through when you've never been hurt," she said.

"The hell I haven't. I was engaged before this. Kylie decided she wanted a man who could give her the money she needed to be happy while not working long hours. She left me, Cathy Jane. Don't tell me about being hurt."

"I'm sorry," she said.

"My mind says don't confess your emotions to this woman but my heart knows not saying the words won't make the hurt lessen."

Tears burned the back of her eyes and a trembling started deep inside her. She was so cold. So damned cold. She wrapped her arms around her body trying to hold herself together but it wasn't working. She was splintering and shattering apart and nothing, no one—not even Tad—could make this right. "I can't stay."

"Why not?"

"Because I'm afraid."

"We've been over this before. I won't hurt you."

She didn't know how to explain to him that she knew he wouldn't intentionally hurt her. But he would all the same. She was an expert at playing the odds when it came to relationships. About understanding how much she could take before fate stepped in and shut her down. He didn't know that for her living with him would be the beginning of the countdown clock.

"Yes, you will. No man has ever stayed once he lived with me. I'm not like other women."

"How many men?"

"Just my dad. And of course there was Marcus."

"Who's Marcus?"

"He was my boss and my fiancé. He left me for a woman more suitable to be the boss's wife."

"I'm not like other men," he said.

No he was like the other half of her soul. And losing him was the one thing she wouldn't risk. "I know."

Tad cursed under his breath. The strength of his words and the anger behind them made her heart break. She glanced around the room. Saw the candles burning in the dining room. Heard the soft romantic music playing on the CD. That he should have gone to so much trouble to prepare this evening for her... "Tad, it's not that I don't care."

"Then what is it, CJ? Because you told me Butch wants you married. I offered you a business arrangement and that wasn't what you wanted. I've offered you love and still that's not good enough. Is it me? Is this some sort of payback for the insensitive boy I was?"

"No. Never. I love you, Tad, in a way I thought never to love another man. But I can't marry you."

"Why not?" he asked again, frustration in every line of his body.

"Because fate won't let me have it all when it comes to men."

"What men?"

"My dad. Marcus. You. Every man I've ever cared for has left me."

"Are you sure?" he asked.

"What do you mean?"

"Maybe you drove them away with your attitude," he said, then pivoted on his heel and crossed the room to the bar.

"I need a drink."

CJ couldn't move. Perhaps he was right and her attitude was responsible for this entire mess. From the time Tad had walked back into her life, she been searching for a way to escape from him. Be it through her contacts and hair color, or her career. Whatever the reason she needed more time than he'd given her. More time than Butch had allotted her and more time than her weary heart had been given. "Maybe you're right and I drove them away."

Tad opened a bottle of Dewar's and poured it into a shot glass. He knocked back two shots before he even glanced her way. "Screw it. I don't care if you love me or not. Marry me."

"Why?" she asked. Why would he still want to marry her unless everything he'd said had been a joke? Oh, God, don't let him be fooling me once again into believing he's better than he has to be.

He poured himself another shot but this time only

sipped it. "I told my parents they'd be meeting my future wife tomorrow."

"How could you do that? I told you how I felt."

"Obviously, I thought I knew how to change your mind," he said, throwing back another shot. He lifted the bottle again and she knew she had to do something. She couldn't stand by and let him drink anymore.

She couldn't stand to see him like this. This was her handiwork. No matter her intentions of protecting them both from heartache. She'd driven Tad to a bottle of Dewar's. The strong man whose only mistake was loving her. She crossed the room and tried to hug him but he shrugged her off.

"Tad, don't do this. I told you I only wanted an affair," she said. She'd known her track record. Understood herself better than Tad ever could. Her fears stemmed from a childhood spent moving from place to place following the trail of a man who didn't want to be found. Love and approval always seemed just out of her reach. She and Marnie had done their best for each other, but the sisters had known that nothing lasted forever and love was very fragile.

"I should have listened to you," he said with a mocking smile that cut her.

She needed to get out of here. Now. "Yes, you should have."

He threw back another shot.

"Drinking's not going to help."

"It might."

"Please, stop. I can't stand to see you this way."

He shrugged his massive shoulders. She knew he could take on many burdens but she'd never been willing to share hers. Even with this man.

"Apparently that's a common feeling for you," he said.

"It isn't." But there he was clearly not listening to her anymore.

"Perhaps, you should go," he said, walking to the dining area and blowing out the candles. He turned off the music with a discreet flick of his wrist.

"Yes, I should."

She had no idea how to make this right but knew staying with Tad wasn't the solution. There was too much in life that wasn't certain. Too many things she couldn't control and the only way she could protect them both was to stop this now.

She walked back across the room, and picked up her purse, which had fallen to the floor. She owed him something, some sort of explanation. "There's something broken inside me, Tad. It's been that way for a long time."

He looked at her with his wizard green eyes sober. "It's going to stay that way until you trust someone—until you trust me."

She wrapped her arms around her waist. Trying to keep it together until she could get back to her place. Until she reached her sanctuary so she could finally let go of all the hurt and dreams she'd secretly been building in her soul. "I don't know that I ever can."

"Because you've been disappointed before? Hell, we all have. Pierce's wife left him when he lost the use of his legs. Does that seem fair to you, CJ?"

"No, it doesn't. But you aren't Pierce and you aren't me. I've lived my life knowing I wasn't good enough for my father. Knowing that I wasn't woman enough to keep my fiancé. Knowing that sooner or later you'd ask me for something I couldn't give you. And I'm afraid I won't do it again."

"I can make you marry me," he said at last. They stood only a few inches apart but she'd put a rift bigger than Lake Michigan between them.

"How?" She had the feeling his words were motivated by ego and a thirst for revenge.

"I could talk to Butch and make marrying me a stipulation of your promotion," he said, a cruel sneer on his lips.

Her stomach knotted. She read the sincerity in him and knew that if he wanted to punish her for rejecting his proposal then he could do it. This wasn't her childhood friend who'd bandaged her scraped knee. This was the boy who'd cruelly told his popular friends that she'd paid him to talk to her. And this Tad was one she hardly knew.

"You wouldn't, would you?"

"That you even have to ask tells me everything I needed to know." He bent down to pull on his shoes and then stood and went to the coat closet. "I've dismissed the car for the evening. So I'll give you a ride home."

"I can take a cab."

"No you can't."

He took her coat and held it out to her. The bouquet of roses he'd sent in the car for her lay scattered on the floor. The Tiffany's box nestled in the middle of the petals. She felt like crying when she saw it. She shivered a little.

She crossed to him and slid her arms in her coat, but still she was chilled. She followed Tad out the door and down the hall. Each step she took was heavy and her heart beat slowly. He drove her to her condo and saw her to her door in a frosty silence that seemed too loud.

"This is it, then," he said. "I'm not coming back again."

"It doesn't have to be this way."

"How can it be, CJ?"

"We could still have an affair."

"No, we couldn't. I require trust from my lovers and you've proven the only person you trust is yourself. Enjoy your lonely life," he said and walked away. She watched until he disappeared around the corner and then sank to the floor and buried her head against her knees. She'd never felt more isolated from the world than she had at that moment.

# Twelve

**CJ** woke Christmas morning feeling more alone than ever. She'd slept fitfully the previous night, plagued by dreams of Tad. Only the knowledge that Rae-Anne was coming over for brunch motivated her to get out of bed.

She entered her kitchen and made coffee first. Opening the refrigerator was a mistake. She'd purchased extra food anticipating the days that Tad would stay with her. For a minute she wanted to say the hell with her fears and go back to his place and beg him to forgive her. But she knew that she'd sabotage their relationship because in her heart she didn't believe it would last.

She didn't want to cook. Instead she climbed up on

the counter and pulled out that box of HoHos. There was only one cure for what ailed her. And that was the sugar-induced euphoria that chocolate cream-filled cakes could bring.

She took them to the living room and sat in front of her Christmas tree with the box. She opened the first cake and took a huge bite. But the cake didn't taste right in her mouth. She opened another package and tried that one. Again something wasn't right with the cake.

She threw the box on the coffee table disgusted with herself. Even her old comfort had been taken. She wanted to cry.

The doorbell rang. She was still in her pajamas. Her hair wasn't combed and she had coffee breath. Oh, God. Rae-Anne was here.

CJ had invited her secretary when she realized Rae-Anne had no family. As she had thought of her aging lonely secretary, CJ realized that could be the life she'd chosen for herself. Maybe she should get a cat.

"Just a minute," she called out.

She grabbed the HoHos and ran for the kitchen. She'd make omelettes or something. She grabbed a hair scrunchy from the basket in the kitchen and twisted her hair into a ponytail. Her flannel pjs weren't really company appropriate but she didn't want to leave Rae-Anne standing in the hall. She opened the door and tried to smile.

Rae-Anne took in her appearance. "What the hell happened to you?"

"Merry Christmas, to you too."

"*Buon Natale*. Is Tad here? Should I have stayed home?"

"No, come in. I'm all alone." The word echoed in her mind.

Rae-Anne placed a present on the hall table and CJ hung her coat up. "Let me run down the hall and change. Make yourself at home. There's coffee in the kitchen."

CJ hurriedly dressed in a pair of black leggings and a long black tunic sweater. She brushed out her hair and twisted it up in a knot. She put in her contacts and applied makeup and when she entered the living room and saw the tree she'd decorated with Tad, she paused for a moment, registering the pain deep inside of her and moved on.

Why couldn't Tad have been content with what they had?

Rae-Anne had made a breakfast of scones, clotted cream and fresh fruit. "Did you bring this food with you?"

"Uh…yeah. Where's Tad this morning?"

"At his home I imagine."

"You don't know?"

"Uh, things kind of didn't work out."

"What? Why not?"

"We just…I'm not…oh, hell. I don't want to talk about it."

"Did he treat you poorly?"

CJ was swamped with memories of how well Tad

had treated her. In bed he was her dream lover. Out of bed he was a surprising mix of macho determination and romantic notions. She'd never forget their dinner at Gejas or walking along State Street and looking at the Christmas windows.

But more than memories lingered. He'd made her feel special and accepted her for who she was. As if he didn't expect anymore or less from her than she was willing to give.

"No."

"Did you have a fight?"

"Yeah, a real doozy. Listen, it just wasn't meant to be. I learned that lesson a long time ago and there's nothing left to say on the matter."

"Why not?"

"I'm just not what Tad needs."

"He told you that?"

"No. He didn't have to. I don't want to talk about him anymore." It was hard enough dealing with all her doubts, fears and recriminations. She didn't want to discuss it with her secretary.

Rae-Anne took a sip of her coffee and then she stood up. "Will Tad take you back?"

"What? Are you listening to me, Rae-Anne? I'm not talking about this anymore."

"*Madon'*, that's what I was afraid of."

"Why do you care?"

Rae-Anne stood up and walked to stand in front of her. "I'm a matchmaker sent from Heaven."

"Give me a break."

"I'm trying to."

"I don't believe this. Have you been drinking?"

"No and neither have you," Rae-Anne said. She took CJ's hand, pulling her to her feet. "Come with me."

"Where are we going?"

"To your future." Rae-Anne snapped her fingers and the walls around them shifted. CJ knew she was having some kind of freaky nightmare as they flew through time.

"I think I'm freaking out," CJ said to herself. She closed her eyes tightly and muttered a prayer under her breath.

"Trust me, you're not."

"Where are we?"

"I don't know. This is the place you brought us to."

CJ pinched her thigh hard and gasped when the pain was real. This wasn't a dream. She stood in front of her childhood home in Auburndale. The yard had one of those tacky chain-link fences around it. The battered Buick Century she and Marnie had shared sat in the driveway. But Rae-Anne didn't lead her up the walk to her house.

"Why did you bring me here?" CJ asked. "I've spent my adult life never looking back at this time."

"Yet this is where your subconscious brought you. Why is that?"

CJ saw her teenaged self—wearing a pair of baggie

jeans and a long T-shirt. Rae-Anne took her hand and they followed that teenaged girl next door. And CJ stopped, refusing to take another step. She knew where they were and what day it was.

"Rae-Anne, let's leave now."

"Can't do it. What's going on here?"

Four days before prom and she'd been making her way over to Tad's place to ask him to go with her. Oh, God. This was her worst memory. No way had she chosen this place to come. No way.

"I don't think this is going to help unless your mission is to make me depressed."

Rae-Anne pulled CJ close in her arms and hugged her. "Of course it isn't. But you need to see this through adult eyes and not from a clouded teenage perspective."

They went around the back of the Randolphs' sprawling ranch house and CJ saw the pool and two boys who were drinking sodas at the table next to it. Tad was skinnier than she remembered him being. She didn't see her teenage self but knew that she'd been hiding behind the hedges out of sight of the boys and listening.

"I called last night and your mom said you were on a date. Did you get back with Patti?" asked Bart Johnson. He'd been the quarterback of their football team and had dated only cheerleaders.

"No. I was out with Cathy Jane Terrence."

CJ remembered that night. They'd gone to see the *Batman* movie and he'd teased her about being like

Michelle Pfeiffer—he'd called her Cat Girl. They'd had a lot of fun that night. She'd forgotten about her hair and weight. For once she'd felt like…a woman worthy of a man's attention.

"Who?" Bart asked. She wasn't surprised to realize he didn't even know her name.

"You know my neighbor." Tad gestured to her house with his Pepsi can.

"That fat girl? Why?"

"Why do you care?" Tad asked.

"I don't. It just makes no sense. You could go out with any girl at school."

"I don't want any girl," Tad said.

"Man, I don't get it."

Tad took a swallow of his drink then said, "She pays me to hang with her."

Bart started laughing and CJ saw her teenage self run by. Back to her house and the box of HoHos waiting there. This she remembered.

"Let's go. I didn't see anything that made a difference."

"We're not done yet," Rae-Anne said.

"How much is she paying you?" Bart asked.

"Man, she doesn't pay me. Did you hit your head on the diving board earlier?"

Bart shook his head and grabbed a handful of chips from the bowl on the table. He picked up his sunglasses and put them on. "I don't understand you. Why do you hang with her?"

Tad rubbed his stomach and glanced toward her

house. She couldn't see him clearly and wished she were closer to him. "She's sweet and I like her smile."

CJ's heart broke all over again. In all the time they'd been together he'd never mentioned this to her. Not that she'd have ever let him talk about it.

"You know what they say about fat girls?" Bart asked.

"What?"

"They're like mopeds—fun to ride until you're around your friends."

Tad punched Bart hard in the arm and Bart fell off balance into the pool. "Hey, man. What was that about?"

"Nothing you'd understand."

Rae-Anne gripped CJ's arm and snapped her fingers. CJ was sitting back at her kitchen table. The food was gone and her coffee cup was in front of her. Still warm. Rae-Anne was nowhere to be found and CJ wondered if she'd dreamed the entire episode.

She sat back in her chair. It didn't matter if it happened or not, she was coming to realize something. Fate was influenced by her perception of reality. She'd always thought she wasn't good enough for the men in her life. When all the time maybe she was projecting those feelings on them.

She stood up and paced her kitchen. She realized she had a choice to make—play it safe and live her life on the sidelines or take a leap. She closed her eyes and realized there really was only one choice.

But was it too late? Could she convince Tad that they could both find the happiness they deserved?

Tad's parents had been delayed in Florida because of bad weather and had decided to delay their visit until after the holidays. Originally, he'd planned to take them to CJ's for dinner. She'd promised to cook a meal he'd never forget. And he'd planned to make the holiday special for her. Well it looked like they both succeeded in making it unforgettable.

He'd spent most of last night in his weight room working out and wondering if he'd ever really understand women. He had a history of pursuing the ones who were most out of reach. And this time it had proved disastrous.

Traditionally, he and Pierce went for a run on Christmas morning. They'd started it the year Karen had divorced Pierce. Wracked with depression Pierce had almost overdosed on prescription medication on Christmas Eve that year. Pierce had dreaded facing the morning alone so Tad had suggested they meet early in the morning and exercise. That was more than eight years ago and they still continued the tradition.

It didn't matter if one or both of them were in relationships. If it was raining or snowing or twenty below—they still met. Some years they simply sat in a hotel lobby, drinking coffee. Other years they ran. Pierce was faster in his wheelchair than Tad, but that didn't matter.

This year, Tad knew he needed exercise. He needed

to run as far as he could until CJ was a distant memory and the pain of her rejection started to heal.

"Merry Christmas, buddy," Pierce said when he joined him in front of the Navy Pier. They started at the Pier and ran north.

"You too," Tad said.

"Tawny's picking me up in an hour. Want to call CJ and we can all go get brunch at the Hilton?"

"Uh, no."

"Why not?"

"CJ and I aren't together anymore. Let's go."

Pierce said nothing, letting Tad set the pace. His feet pounding on the pavement providing the rhythm of his thoughts, but the exercise wasn't helping. Nevertheless he kept going and finally they arrived back at the pier. Tawny was waiting out front with a couple of cups of hot tea. Tad slowed and then stopped.

He watched his friend pick up his woman and put her on his lap. Pierce bent close to Tawny and she laughed. And Tad felt a longing deep in his soul. He finally admitted to himself that he'd wanted marriage not because his mom and dad were getting older and wanted grandkids. He was getting older and needed the grounding that only a soul mate and a family could provide.

Tad also admitted that he hadn't really trusted CJ enough to let her all the way into his life. He'd been protecting part of himself from her. So that in case she left he'd still have a part that was untouched by her.

He waved goodbye to Pierce and Tawny and returned to his condo. He took the stairs instead of the elevator because he was too restless to wait for the lift. His mind was going fifty miles an hour and he wondered if he could convince CJ to start again.

He realized he'd pushed too hard and fast for something that neither of them were ready to admit they wanted.

He slowed his pace when he entered his floor. Someone was waiting on his doorstep. "CJ?"

"Can I talk to you?" She seemed hesitant and he didn't blame her. Her hair was twisted up and she had those damned blue contacts in again. He was disappointed deep inside.

He wished she'd give up the costumes and play-acting and come to him as herself. He unlocked his door and stepped inside. The jewelry box still sat on the hall table. He glanced at her and saw that she was staring at it.

He tossed his keys on the table and went into the kitchen to put some coffee on. She followed him into the room. Even though he didn't face her, he knew exactly where she was.

"What do you want?"

"Um…I wanted to…" She walked over to him. He heard her footsteps on his ceramic tile floor. Her touch on his shoulder was light and tentative. He didn't turn. She took his shoulder and forced him to face her. He leaned back against the counter and crossed his arms over his chest. He hadn't expected his arms to feel empty when he saw her again. He hadn't expected the longing to hold her would be so strong. He hadn't expected her to brand his soul as thoroughly as she had.

"Please. This is hard enough for me."

"I haven't exactly had an easy time of it."

"I know. Listen I'm sorry about last night."

"You came over to apologize."

"Not exactly."

He arched one eyebrow at her and waited.

This was more difficult than she'd thought it would be and she realized that was because she was still afraid to really risk her heart. She took a deep breath.

"I want you, Tad."

"Not too badly."

"Why do you say that?"

"You're wearing your contacts, CJ."

"What?"

"You think I don't know that you use that upswept hairdo and those colored contacts to hide from the world. I showed you my soul. I bared myself to you last night—confessed things to you that I've never said to another person and still you're not willing to meet me as an equal."

"Is that what you think?" she asked.

He had nothing left to lose with her. "I know it."

"Fine," she said. Reaching up she pulled the pins from her hair and then took out her contacts. Then she surprised him by removing every stitch of her clothing.

"This is it, Tad. The real me standing before you without any shields, without any barriers."

He ached for her. "Why?"

"Because I'm not really living life and I can't stand the thought that I'll miss out on sharing my days with you."

"Why this sudden change of heart?"

She crossed her arms over her chest and he knew how vulnerable she must feel standing naked in front of him. He wanted to pull her into his arms and protect her but first he had to be sure she wanted him to protect her.

"I was running from my feelings and the uncertainty that comes with love. But not anymore. The only thing I fear is not ever waking up with you again."

He was humbled by her sincerity and the risk she took with her heart.

"Please say something."

"Come here," he said, opening his arms. She walked into them and he hugged her tight.

"I love you," she said, standing on tiptoe and whispering into his ear. "I want to spend the rest of my life with you."

Tad scooped her up in his arms and bent to kiss her. He walked down the hall to his bedroom. He placed her in the center of his bed. "Wait here."

He went back to the foyer and grabbed the engagement ring. He returned to find the woman he loved waiting for him. And realized deep in his soul that he'd found the kind of happiness he'd never really believed existed before this.

He felt like he'd been sucker punched by his emotions. ''God, I love you, Cathy Jane.''

''Come to bed and prove it,'' she said with a saucy grin.

''Not yet.'' He climbed onto the bed and sat next to her hips. He ran his hand down her body from neck to belly button and back again.

Her breathing grew heavier and her skin was flushed. He saw the signs of arousal on her breasts and bent to drop short kisses on each of her nipples.

''Ah, I need you,'' she said.

But he pulled back, he wanted her to be wearing his ring the next time he made her his. He pulled the ring from the box.

''Will you marry me?''

She smiled up at him, tears glistening in her eyes. ''I will.''

He put the ring on her finger and kissed her deeply. He made love to her with an intensity that left them both trembling. Afterwards tucked under the covers of his bed, he held her in his arms and they made plans for the future. And Tad knew that he'd found a treasure greater than gold in the woman in his arms.

# Epilogue

"**N**ot bad, Mandetti," Didi said appearing beside me.

I was standing outside Tad's condo congratulating myself on getting another couple together. I'd had my doubts for a while that they would do it. But in the end a little angel magic had done the trick. "Hey, babe, what'd you expect from the King of Hearts."

The angel broad moved around to stand next to me. She wore another one of her ugly dresses but this one was in a yellow color that didn't look too bad. *Madon'* I must be getting soft.

"You're not a capo anymore, Pasquale."

I hated when she called me by my given name. "Maybe not like I used to be."

"You like matchmaking," she said.

"It beats the alternative." Which was me going to hell. God knows I'd have deserved it if they'd sent me there.

She smiled at me. What was she up to? "Yes, it does."

"This time wasn't too bad except for you making me a dame. I ain't doing that again."

"Who says you get a choice?" Didi asked.

"Babe, you are some piece of work."

She laughed. "Mandetti, what have I told you about calling me babe?"

"If I stop can I be a guy next time?"

"Maybe," she said and disappeared.

That one was always trying to drive me crazy. I'd never tell her but I liked doing good deeds. CJ had needed me as a friend and I'd never really been there for anyone before. I wished I'd done it for Tess when she'd been in my life. I was sounding like a *babbeo*.

But then there was something crazy about this love business. And though I'd never admit it to Didi I liked my new gig.

\* \* \* \* \*

*Turn the page for a bonus look at the next title in Katherine Garbera's*
**KING OF HEARTS** *miniseries:*
*1558 LET IT RIDE*
*by Katherine Garbera*
*January 2004*

Introducing a brand-new series from

# Katherine Garbera

### You're on his hit list.

What do the mob and happily-ever-after have in
common? A matchmaking ex-gangster who's been
given one last chance to go straight. To get into heaven
he must unite couples in love. As he works to earn his
angel's wings, find out who his next targets are.

### IN BED WITH BEAUTY
**(Silhouette Desire #1535)**
**On sale September 2003**

### CINDERELLA'S CHRISTMAS AFFAIR
**(Silhouette Desire #1546)**
**On sale November 2003**

### LET IT RIDE
**(Silhouette Desire #1558)**
**On sale January 2004**

*Available at your favorite retail outlet.*

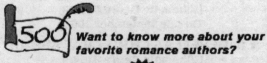

**Your opinion is important to us!** Please take a few moments to share your thoughts with us about your experiences with Harlequin and Silhouette books. Your comments will be very useful in ensuring that we deliver books you love to read. *Please take a few minutes to complete the questionnaire, then send it to us at the address below.*

---

Send your completed questionnaires to:
**Harlequin/Silhouette Reader Survey, P.O. Box 9046, Buffalo, NY 14269-9046**

---

1. As you may know, there are many different lines under the Harlequin and Silhouette brands. Each of the lines is listed below. Please check the box that most represents your reading habit for each line.

| Line | Currently read this line | Do not read this line | Not sure if I read this line |
|---|---|---|---|
| Harlequin American Romance | ❏ | ❏ | ❏ |
| Harlequin Duets | ❏ | ❏ | ❏ |
| Harlequin Romance | ❏ | ❏ | ❏ |
| Harlequin Historicals | ❏ | ❏ | ❏ |
| Harlequin Superromance | ❏ | ❏ | ❏ |
| Harlequin Intrigue | ❏ | ❏ | ❏ |
| Harlequin Presents | ❏ | ❏ | ❏ |
| Harlequin Temptation | ❏ | ❏ | ❏ |
| Harlequin Blaze | ❏ | ❏ | ❏ |
| Silhouette Special Edition | ❏ | ❏ | ❏ |
| Silhouette Romance | ❏ | ❏ | ❏ |
| Silhouette Intimate Moments | ❏ | ❏ | ❏ |
| Silhouette Desire | ❏ | ❏ | ❏ |

2. Which of the following best describes why you bought *this book?* One answer only, please.

| | | | |
|---|---|---|---|
| the picture on the cover | ❏ | the title | ❏ |
| the author | ❏ | the line is one I read often | ❏ |
| part of a miniseries | ❏ | saw an ad in another book | ❏ |
| saw an ad in a magazine/newsletter | ❏ | a friend told me about it | ❏ |
| I borrowed/was given this book | ❏ | other: _____ | ❏ |

3. Where did you buy *this book?* One answer only, please.

| | | | |
|---|---|---|---|
| at Barnes & Noble | ❏ | at a grocery store | ❏ |
| at Waldenbooks | ❏ | at a drugstore | ❏ |
| at Borders | ❏ | on eHarlequin.com Web site | ❏ |
| at another bookstore | ❏ | from another Web site | ❏ |
| at Wal-Mart | ❏ | Harlequin/Silhouette Reader | ❏ |
| at Target | ❏ | Service/through the mail | |
| at Kmart | ❏ | used books from anywhere | ❏ |
| at another department store or mass merchandiser | ❏ | I borrowed/was given this book | ❏ |

4. On average, how many Harlequin and Silhouette books do you buy at one time?

| | |
|---|---|
| I buy _____ books at one time | ❏ |
| I rarely buy a book | ❏ |

MRQ403SD-1A

5. How many times per month do you shop for any *Harlequin and/or Silhouette* books?
   One answer only, please.

   | | | | |
   |---|---|---|---|
   | 1 or more times a week | ❑ | a few times per year | ❑ |
   | 1 to 3 times per month | ❑ | less often than once a year | ❑ |
   | 1 to 2 times every 3 months | ❑ | never | ❑ |

6. When you think of your ideal heroine, which *one* statement describes her the best?
   One answer only, please.

   | | | | |
   |---|---|---|---|
   | She's a woman who is strong-willed | ❑ | She's a desirable woman | ❑ |
   | She's a woman who is needed by others | ❑ | She's a powerful woman | ❑ |
   | She's a woman who is taken care of | ❑ | She's a passionate woman | ❑ |
   | She's an adventurous woman | | She's a sensitive woman | ❑ |

7. The following statements describe types or genres of books that you may be
   interested in reading. Pick *up to 2 types* of books that you are most interested in.

   | | |
   |---|---|
   | I like to read about truly romantic relationships | ❑ |
   | I like to read stories that are sexy romances | ❑ |
   | I like to read romantic comedies | ❑ |
   | I like to read a romantic mystery/suspense | ❑ |
   | I like to read about romantic adventures | ❑ |
   | I like to read romance stories that involve family | ❑ |
   | I like to read about a romance in times or places that I have never seen | ❑ |
   | Other: _____ | ❑ |

*The following questions help us to group your answers with those readers who are
similar to you. Your answers will remain confidential.*

8. Please record your year of birth below.
   19 _____

9. What is your marital status?

   | | | | | | | | |
   |---|---|---|---|---|---|---|---|
   | single | ❑ | married | ❑ | common-law | ❑ | widowed | ❑ |
   | divorced/separated | ❑ | | | | | | |

10. Do you have children 18 years of age or younger currently living at home?

    yes ❑          no ❑

11. Which of the following best describes your employment status?

    | | | | | | |
    |---|---|---|---|---|---|
    | employed full-time or part-time | ❑ | homemaker | ❑ | student | ❑ |
    | retired | ❑ | unemployed | ❑ | | |

12. Do you have access to the Internet from either home or work?

    yes ❑          no ❑

13. Have you ever visited eHarlequin.com?

    yes ❑          no ❑

14. What state do you live in?

    _____

15. Are you a member of Harlequin/Silhouette Reader Service?

    yes ❑     Account # _____     no     ❑     MRQ403SD-1B

# COMING NEXT MONTH